SIBÉAL POUNDER

Illustrated by
Laura Ellen
Anderson

BLOOMSBURY
CHILDREN'S BOOKS
LONDON OXFORD NEW YORK NEW DELHI SYDNEY

BLOOMSBURY CHILDREN'S BOOKS
Bloomsbury Publishing Plc
50 Bedford Square, London WC1B 3DP, UK

BLOOMSBURY, BLOOMSBURY CHILDREN'S BOOKS and the Diana logo are trademarks of Bloomsbury Publishing Plc

First published in Great Britain in 2018 by Bloomsbury Publishing Plc

A catalogue record for this book is available from the British Library

ISBN: PB: 978-1-4088-9412-5; eBook: 978-1-4088-9411-8

2 4 6 8 10 9 7 5 3

Typeset by RefineCatch Limited, Bungay, Suffolk
Printed and bound in Great Britain by CPI Group (UK) Ltd, Croydon CR0 4YY

To find out more about our authors and books visit www.bloomsbury.com and sign up for our newsletters

For James, Emily and Arthur

THE BADLANDS
THE DOCKS
DESPERATE DOLLS
DRIPTOWN
THE LAKES
SINKVILLE EXPRESS
TRAIN STATION
LINDEN HOUSE
RITZY CITY
SILVER CITY
Clutterbucks
CAKES, PIES & THAT'S ABOUT IT REALLY
GULL & CHIP TAVERN
RITZY CITY
JAM & CATS
JAM

SINKVILLE
THE COVES
WAVERLY WAY
PEARL PEAK
PEARL PEAK ACADEMY
FOREST
LITTLE LEAF RESTAURANT
WHERE THE FIRST WITCH LANDED IN SINKVILLE
BROLLYWOOD
FAIRY CARAVAN PARK
THE CAULDRON ISLANDS
BUBBLE BEACH
THE OLD CAULDRON FACTORY
THE TOWERS

The Story So Far

Last time in Ritzy City:

Since falling into the witchy world of Sinkville, Tiga has had her fair share of adventures – from competing in Witch Wars and stopping Celia Crayfish taking over Sinkville, to saving Fran from vats of jam and keeping Lucy Tatty, her number one fan, at bay. But she's had her best friends by her side and together they are fabulously powerful ... which is lucky, because they are about to face their most dangerous adventure yet.

1

No, Fran!

Patricia the producer had said no to Fran's suggestions almost every day since the day they met. She had said no when Fran had come up with a new rule called BEEHIVES OR BOOING on all Brollywood TV shows and films.

'Any actor not sporting a beehive hairstyle like mine is booed – non-stop,' Fran had explained enthusiastically before Patricia the producer told her to get out of her office.

Patricia the producer had also said NO when Fran had come up with a new game show called *Whack-a-Witch*.

'You take a big mallet and then you –'

'NO!' Patricia the producer shouted.

But today was different. Fran had a new idea for a TV show – something fairy-filled and fabulous. Something that would send all of Sinkville into a frenzy. It would be bigger than *Cooking for Tiny People*, bigger even than *Witch Wars*.

And big enough to distract everyone in town from something awful that was headed their way …

The Points Are Calling

Two weeks later, Tiga and Fluffanora sat on the floor in Brew's.

'*Fairy Fights?*' Tiga said flatly. 'That's what Fran called it?'

'With a *Z*,' Fluffanora said, not looking up. She was flicking her finger back and forth, sewing a sharp cuff on a tiny glittering jumpsuit. 'They say it's going to be the biggest show Sinkville has ever seen. And also the tiniest because it's an all-fairy cast.'

'Why are you designing the costumes?' Tiga asked, lifting up a long one with extra-large wing holes cut out of the back.

'That one's for Julie Jumbo Wings,' Fluffanora said,

spinning the jumpsuit slowly in a circle with her finger, inspecting every detail. 'Perfect!'

She flicked her finger and snipped the thread.

'They asked my mum to do them, but she didn't have time. She's busy making a new Ritzy City hat design for some visiting mermaid queen. She's gone to Driptown to deliver the hat designs to the Mermaid Museum – she had to create five different options. I told her to go crazy with the shells.'

'My mum's in Driptown too,' Tiga said. 'Working on the royal visit, only she's fixing the magic bathtub invention that they use to transport the mermaid – Ooh!'

She waved a copy of the *Ritzy City Post* in Fluffanora's face.

'Look!' she said. 'They're running daily exclusives about Fran's new show – this one has an interview with Fran in it and –'

She stopped when she saw two envelopes march through the door.

Fluffanora scooped them up. 'Strange. They're usually

for my mum. I never really get post, unless you send me a note, but you're here. Wait – Tiga, this one's for you! It must've followed you here.'

Tiga ripped it open. She rarely got post either, apart from fan letters from Lucy Tatty.

Tiga, you have been selected for an interview to join the Points.
Come to the forest. Five footsteps to the left of the Little Leaf Café.
Tonight at the first sign of dark.
Be there.

'Mine says the same,' Fluffanora said, staring at Tiga's note.

'But why would the Points choose *us*?' Tiga mumbled as she read the letter again. The Points were a group of secretive and cool witches who went to Pearl Peak High. *Everyone* wanted to find out what happened at their secret meetings. It was rumoured Felicity Bat's big sister,

Idabelle, was in charge. Tiga stared down at the letter excitedly.

'We should go,' Fluffanora said, obviously thinking the same thing. 'I don't want to be in their club, but it would be fun to see what the fuss is about. I want to know what happens at the secret meetings.'

Tiga looked up. 'Do you think Felicity Bat got an invite?'

'I absolutely did not!' Felicity Bat said angrily. Peggy came clattering into the Linden House sitting room with a tray of Clutterbucks cocktails. She tripped and fell head first into the sofa. Felicity Bat flicked her finger, halting Peggy before she made contact with it.

'Thanks!' Peggy said cheerily, as Felicity Bat flicked her finger again, making a pillow leap up and smack Peggy in the face.

'I've always wanted to go to a secret Points gathering,' Felicity Bat went on, inspecting the letter before

throwing it back at Fluffanora. 'She's doing this to make me jealous.'

'Why would she do that?' Fluffanora said.

'Because it's *Idabelle*. My sister lives to make my life miserable.'

'Then *why*,' Fluffanora said pointedly, 'do you want to be in her club?'

'I DON'T KNOW!' Felicity Bat roared, before levitating out of the room at the speed of a slug. 'But you shouldn't go.'

'Why is she going so slowly?' Tiga whispered to Peggy.

'She got new boots,' Peggy whispered back.

'I like the sparkly tips on the toes,' Tiga said. 'But they aren't Felicity Bat's style *at all*.'

'And they're too heavy, I think,' Peggy added. 'They weigh her down. I have no idea why she insists on wearing them. It's strange. I suppose she can just take them off if she needs to get somewhere in a rush.'

Tiga looked over and saw Fluffanora fold up the letter and slip it into her skirt pocket.

'So are you going to go?' Peggy asked. 'I'd go if I was invited!'

'Obviously,' Fluffanora butted in. 'I'm intrigued. And so is Tiga, though she's not admitting it.'

Tiga frowned. 'I wish you could come too, Peggy.'

'Just be careful,' Peggy said. 'If you think Felicity Bat can be cunning, you should hear some of the stories about Idabelle.'

Fairy Fightz Rehearsal

'*Fairy Fightz! Fairy Fightz!*

Scrunch up your fists and put glitter on your cheeks for …

Fairy Fightz! Fairy Fightz!' came Fran's singing from her caravan.

'That can't be the theme tune,' Crispy the fairy grumbled from behind a tiny desk inside.

Fran stopped singing and drooped in the air. 'Why not?'

'Because it's DREADFUL.'

Fran threw her arms in the air and huffed. 'Crispy! Stop buzzing around my head being negative!'

'I'm not even buzzing!' Crispy said angrily. 'I'm DESKBOUND.'

She hit the desk with her fist but Fran was already distracted, peering eagerly out of the tiny window.

'The others are here with the costumes!' Fran squealed. 'Did I tell you they were made by Fluffanora Brew?'

'Only a few hundred times,' Crispy said as she rolled up some tiny pieces of paper and tucked them under her arm.

A massive wing smacked against the caravan window.

'JULIE JUMBO WINGS, YOU ARE GOING TO BREAK MY WINDOW!' Fran bellowed, making the caravan shake.

'Very sorry!' they heard Julie Jumbo Wings say outside, in a tone that didn't sound like she was very sorry at all.

☆☆☆

Patricia the producer arrived on set at the fairy caravan park two hours later, eager to see how things were going on the new fairy wrestling show.

'WHAT IN ALL WITCHINESS IS GOING ON?' she cried.

Fran was wearing a glittery jumpsuit with a glittery mask strapped across her face (mostly to keep her glasses on when she did extreme backflips, but also as a fashion statement), and she had Julie Jumbo Wings' jumbo wings in her mouth.

'Mufing,' Fran said sheepishly.

Crispy, who was hovering at the edge of the set, nudged Patricia the producer to be quiet. It was an impressive though incredibly small set, with the ring designed to look like a giant rainbow, with glittering stars and high-rise buildings surrounding it.

Donna the fairy came bursting on to the set. She flew straight through one of the buildings, before swinging on Fran's feet, doing a mid-air backflip and wrenching Julie Jumbo Wings from Fran's toothy grasp.

'MWAHAHAHA! I AM TINY FISTS, AND I AM EVIL! I WILL SUCK THE GLITTERY DUST FROM THIS WORLD AND MAKE IT DARK! WITH MY PARTNER IN CRIME – THE GREAT, THE POWERFUL ... FLAPPY!'

'We're still in discussions about the names,' Crispy whispered quickly to Patricia the producer.

Donna – or Tiny Fists – breathed in, making Fran double over as a stream of glittery dust floated out from somewhere in her beehive.

'NO!' Fran cried, clutching her heart and falling through the air, landing with a dramatic thud.

Donna and Julie Jumbo Wings flew off, cackling.

'I MUST STOP THEM!' Fran breathed helplessly, trying to get to her feet. 'I AM THE HERO! THE LEGEND! YOU ALL WANT TO BUY THE LIMITED-EDITION PICTURES OF MY FACE! I AM … THE *ME*!' She limply flopped back on to a star and the stage lights went out.

'And cut,' Crispy said flatly. 'Good scene, everyone.'

'This is going to be huge,' Patricia the producer said, clapping excitedly as Fran got to her feet and bowed.

'She keeps adding the bit about the pictures of her face,' Crispy moaned.

'NOT. NOW. CRISPY,' Fran said. 'Let's not

interrupt Patricia the producer's adoring clapping.'

'I've moved your show forward to tonight – we have a big gap in the schedule because Washy Cat has been balded.'

'Balded?' Fran said, blinking.

'Someone did a shave spell near the Washy Cat costume. There's not a hairy thing left in the costume cupboard.'

Fran bit her lip. 'Oh dear … who would do a thing like that?'

Crispy's mouth fell open and she raised a finger towards Fran. 'It was yo–'

Fran flew straight at her and knocked her off the set. 'Crispy! *Clumsy little thing*.'

'We'll go live in a few hours,' Patricia the producer said, pacing excitedly. 'You'll need extra lights for the set, it's getting dark. Be ready. Nothing must go wrong.'

'Obviously not,' Fran said, not knowing that five minutes deeper into the forest, the stage was set for something to go very wrong indeed.

Idabelle Bat

Tiga trudged through the forest behind Fluffanora, their boots making squelching noises as they went.

'Felicity Bat is going to kill us if she finds out we came here,' Tiga whispered.

'Well, we should remember never to tell her then,' Fluffanora whispered back.

Tiga hopped over a puddle. 'You don't think it's … dangerous, do you?'

'Oh, come on,' Fluffanora said dismissively. 'They're *teenagers*, not monsters.'

'Look,' Tiga said, stopping. 'I see the lights from the fairy caravan park. Maybe we should let Fran know we're here. You know, in case we find

ourselves in any sort of trouble.'

Fluffanora grabbed her arm and ducked behind a bush as Patricia the producer sailed past with her flying umbrella.

'Are you mad?' she whispered. 'The Points is a top-secret society. We can't just wander through the forest merrily telling everyone where we're going. Plus Fran would insist on coming and we'd be thrown out straight away.'

'Good point,' Tiga said, getting to her feet and dusting the leaves and twigs off her tights. She took the invite out of her pocket and studied it again. 'Do you think we're nearly there?'

Fluffanora stopped in front of a line of five identical trees and stood with her hands clasped neatly behind her back.

'What are you doing?' Tiga whispered.

'Just do the same,' Fluffanora said.

Tiga reluctantly did so, staring up at the spindly trees. How could they all be *identical*? she wondered.

'I read about this in *Toad* magazine once,' Fluffanora

said with a wink. 'They did a Points exposé! Although they only got this far and then Idabelle zapped the reporter with some sort of sleeping spell. She's been asleep and dribbling ever since.' She pointed to a glass box to the left of the trees. Tiga could see it contained an unconscious witch. 'They call her Beauty.'

The sleeping witch let out a monstrous snore.

'Luckily the reporter had a magic notebook recording everything that was going on. Mavis found it and posted it back to *Toad* headquarters, thinking someone had lost it. They still couldn't un-zap her though ...'

The sleeping witch let out another monstrous snore.

Tiga looked back to the trees. 'Is something meant to hap–'

BANG!

The puff of smoke made Tiga's eyes sting. And just like that, where the five trees had been seconds earlier, stood five witches in pointy hats.

'Ah,' Idabelle said, marching forward. 'You're right on time.'

5

Felicity Bat Talks to Her Boot

Felicity Bat sat in her den at Linden House. She had her favourite spider cuddly toys and her latest stack of reading material from the Linden House library arranged in a neat pile.

Her left foot began shaking.

'I'm taking them off, hang on,' she said, removing the boot and sticking her face in it. 'It's the safest place for you,' she whispered. 'Just until we can figure out what to do with you.'

The boot shook again.

'All right, I'll get some food. Do you eat jam?'

So You Want to Be in the Points ...

'So you want to be in the Points,' Idabelle Bat said with a smirk.

'Actually,' Tiga began, 'we just –'

Fluffanora kicked her. 'Yes. We *really* do.'

Idabelle gestured to her friends to sit down on the black rocks that encircled a roaring green fire.

A witch in a mermaid-print jumper and slouchy black trousers pushed Tiga out of the way and plonked herself down.

'I'm Melodie McDamp,' she said, extending a hand up to Tiga, who was shifting awkwardly, unsure whether she was meant to sit down too.

'Hi.' Tiga shook it. 'We've met, remember? At the

Mermaid Museum? You work there, don't you?'

'I do, but I don't remember you,' Melodie said with a shrug. 'Wait, do you know Fran? She visits all the time, and last week she stole a plastic lobster.'

'I'm sure she just borrowed it,' Tiga said. 'There's probably a good reason for her taking it.'

Melodie chewed loudly on her gum and blew a huge black bubble that popped in Tiga's face.

Idabelle pointed at the witch next to her. She was small, with a little black bob and a fringe that covered her eyes like sinister curtains.

'This is Bertha Bram. She's secretary of the Points.'

'What does the secretary do?' Fluffanora asked.

'Mostly, I buy snacks,' Bertha said, whipping out a tray of sludgy jam things. 'Star-shaped jam?'

Fluffanora grabbed one in each hand and stuffed them in her mouth. 'Mmm, that tastes really nice.'

'It's special jam – one hundred years old, from the ancient jam stores near the tip of Pearl Peak.'

Fluffanora grabbed another one. 'Mell mere

mexcellent,' she mumbled as jam oozed from the sides of her mouth.

'Well, sit down, Tiga!' Idabelle snapped, making Tiga leap on to the rock like a well-trained frog.

Idabelle pointed to the witch on the other side of Tiga. 'And this witch-shaped wonder is Francesca Fignettle. She's our newest recruit.'

Francesca Fignettle grabbed Tiga by the collar and threw her off the rock.

'What did you do that for?' Tiga cried.

'You were sitting on my spirit rabbit,' Francesca said furiously, scooping some air in her hands and stroking it, as if she were cradling a small animal.

'Spirit rabbit?' Tiga said quietly.

Melodie leaned over.

'Just don't kick her spirit cat,' she whispered. 'She *hates* that.'

Tiga glanced around nervously, then pulled her knees up under her chin and placed her boots firmly on the rock.

'And don't get me started on her spirit *snake*,' Melodie said, blowing another bubble and letting it pop loudly.

'So, Tiga, Fluffanora, you already know Melodie,' Idabelle said, pointing her finger around the circle and coming to a stop at the last witch. 'This is Catriona Catcat.'

'Catcat?' Tiga said with a giggle. 'As in feline feline?'

'Her family invented the spell that turns witches into cats,' Idabelle said. '*Obviously*.'

'My family then changed their name to Catcat,' Catriona explained snootily.

'Why not just go with Cat?' Tiga asked. 'Why Cat*cat*?'

'Because we invented two award-winning cat spells.'

'If your family invent another spell to do with cats, will you become Catriona Catcatcat?' Fluffanora asked, as she tried to stifle a snort.

Catriona stared up at the trees, thinking hard. 'Hmm, I'm not sure ...'

'Well, just don't invent too many cat spells or else

you'll be Catriona Catcatcatcatcatcatcatcatcatcatcat!' Tiga said, practically rolling off her rock in a fit of giggles. When she came up for air she saw everyone glaring at her, apart from Fluffanora, who was purple in the face from trying not to laugh.

'That's *not* funny,' Catriona Catcat said through gritted teeth. 'Why did we invite them, Idabelle?'

'Oh, come on, it was a bit funny,' Idabelle said, waving her hand and turning the green flames of the fire to black.

Patricia the producer came flying past again, this time next to Crispy.

'I told Fran she wasn't allowed real rainbows for the set,' she huffed. 'Those things are expensive and Fran never returns them in one piece. You wouldn't *believe* how much the fines are for broken rainbows.'

Fluffanora dived to the ground and covered her head.

Melodie blew a bubble so big it almost touched Patricia the producer's face.

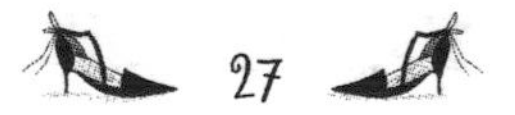

'They can't see us,' Idabelle said with a smirk. 'We use advanced magic to keep our secret meeting place hidden. When they look at us all they can see are trees.'

Crispy turned her head and stared straight at Tiga. Her wings slowed. Tiga looked to see if Fluffanora had noticed too, but she was climbing back on to her stool. She was *positive* Crispy could see her. She was looking straight at them!

'Now,' Idabelle said. 'Let's begin. As per Points rules, we each tell a spooky story.'

'But I haven't prepared anything,' Tiga said.

'Francesca will go first and that'll give you time to think,' Idabelle said. 'You tell a spooky story, and then we vote. If it's good, you're in. If it's not, you're out. We all have to agree.'

Fluffanora rubbed her hands together. Spooky stories were her speciality. She could always be counted on to terrify everyone at a sleepover. Peggy said she'd never look at a toilet the same way after Fluffanora told the Flush Parrot tale.

Francesca stood up and walked straight into the fire.

'What's she doing?!' Tiga cried, but the flames didn't burn Francesca to a crisp. Instead, they swirled up around her, creating a strange seat. She hovered above them, suspended in the fire.

'Whoa,' Tiga breathed.

'My spooky story,' Francesca Fignettle said, 'is about an old ghost called Gordon. He bought a hat with "HUGGABLE" written on it – even though he wasn't huggable. It was confusing, because everything went through him – witches, walls, whining people – but the hat sat *right on his head*. How? And how did he hand over the money for the hat when he couldn't hold sinkels? Now *that's* spooky.'

'NEXT!' Idabelle shouted, rolling her eyes.

TOP STORIES TODAY: THE RITZY SIX ARE ON THE LOOSE, AND A NEW RITZY CITY CAFÉ, CLUTTERBUCKS, OPENS ITS DOORS FOR THE FIRST TIME.

A new and exclusive café called Clutterbucks has opened for the first time! Owned by the Clutterbuck sisters and conveniently located just off of Ritzy Avenue, the place looks set to be a hit with delicious cakes and a menu of bubbling things that they call Clutterbucks cocktails. Entry is exclusively granted by the Clutterbucks themselves and no evil witches will be allowed.

Now on to more pressing matters. Our one and only reporter interviews local Ritzy residents about the threat they face from the devious Ritzy Six gang.

Reporter: We are here with young Mavis, who dreams of opening her own jam stall when she grows up. Mavis, what's been happening with the Ritzy Six?

Mavis: Oh, they've been dreadful – causing all sorts of trouble. They each possess a rare magical talent and are being really disruptive.

Reporter: Now, they go by the names One, Two, Three, Four, Five and Six. Can you tell us what their talents are?

Mavis: Yes. Their talents are: Air, Fire, Water, Earth, Jam, Hair.

Reporter: I am most afraid of the hair one.

Mavis: For me it's the jam one. They keep splatting it everywhere and soon every witch in Sinkville is going to hate jam, thus destroying my future career ambitions.

Reporter: Have the Ritzy Six targeted you?

Mavis: Yes, One, whose power is air, blew me on to the roof of the Ritzytwig Theatre, and I was stuck up there. Everyone thought it was a play and gathered around to watch. I performed for five solid days until someone realised I was actually in distress.

Reporter: And what is the worst thing you've heard about the Ritzy Six?

Mavis: Well, the fairy thing, definitely. Imagine! Wanting to eat fairies! The poor things have had to go into hiding, because if they eat them, the Ritzy Six believe they will become immortal. There are plans to capture and trap the Ritzy Six. My suggestion is that we put them in a jam jar! I'd be willing to look after it.

Reporter: Thank you, Mavis, and good luck with your jam stall dreams.

A FINAL NOTE FROM OUR REPORTER: Please do not try to eat a fairy. Mostly because the small bits on their wings will get stuck in your teeth, and it's the olden days so dentist witches haven't been invented yet.

IN OTHER NEWS: Fairy breaks rainbow and is ordered to pay one million sinkels.

7

Fairy Fightz Goes Live

'Welcome!' came Crispy's less than enthusiastic voice from behind the camera. 'To *FAIRY FIGHTZ*.'

A glitter cannon exploded at the side of the stage as two fairies flew into the tiny wrestling ring. Cardboard rainbows hung around it at lazy angles.

Fran flew to her corner and sat with her arms tightly crossed. 'The real rainbows were much better. Couldn't we –?'

'NO, Fran,' Patricia the producer hissed.

'Today,' Crispy went on, 'something is stirring in the Fairy Realm! A villain! A criminal! A really, really bad thing! She's here to destroy the world!'

Julie Jumbo Wings flew around shaking her fists and flapping her wings, knocking bits off the set as she went.

'This is the evil, evil Flaaaaaaaaaaaaaaaappy!'

The crowd of witches surrounding the tiny stage booed – and all around Sinkville, where witches were watching on the backs of spoons, they booed too.

'Her Jumbo wings wouldn't be able to break *real* rainbows,' Fran said, but Patricia the producer pretended not to hear her.

'But! There is hope. A saviour! A fabulous fairy!'

Patricia the producer stood behind Crispy nodding as Fran waved grandly at the crowds.

'It's … PEEEEEEANNNNUUUUT!'

Fran stopped dead in her tracks and Julie Jumbo Wings ploughed into the back of her. She glared at Crispy.

'I thought her stage name was going to be Her Fabulousness or Fairy God?' Patricia the producer whispered.

'We agreed to change it to Peanut at the last minute,' Crispy lied, her grin growing wider. 'Fran *loves* it.'

'Pea-nut! Pea-nut! Pea-nut! Pea-nut!' the crowd chanted, as Fran reluctantly flew on.

The fairies met in the middle of the ring and pretended to attack each other. Flappy flapped in Peanut's face. Peanut whacked Flappy with her beehive.

'You can do it, Peanut!' the crowd cheered.

'Destroy her, Flappy!' one witch cried.

'DON'T CHEER FOR FLAPPY!' Peanut roared. 'SHE'S THE RUBBISH VILLAIN!'

Peanut got Flappy in a headlock. The lights dimmed.

'Oh no!' came Crispy's voice. 'It looks like Flappy's called for backup.'

A bead of glittery sweat ran down Peanut's face as Flappy shot free of her grasp, flew down to the ground and high-fived … Donna!

The crowd went wild as Donna the fairy, wearing a tutu and a hairband with two glittery fists on springs, took a deep bow.

'IT'S TINY FISTS!' Crispy bellowed.

'Fly, Donna,' Julie Jumbo Wings whispered as

Donna walked lazily across the wrestling ring.

'What? Just because I'm a fairy I have to *fly*? Give me a break!'

Donna promptly lay down and fell asleep.

'You're meant to fly,' Julie Jumbo Wings said in disbelief. 'It's in the script.'

Peanut laughed and grabbed Flappy, flinging her across the stage, into one of the cardboard rainbows.

'POWERFUL ME!' Peanut cried as she twirled up and tied Flappy's wings together.

'None of this is in the script!' Julie Jumbo Wings protested.

There was a huge bang, and the ground began to rumble.

'What was our budget for this?' Patricia the producer asked Crispy. 'That sound effect sounded expensive – and how did you make the ground rumble?'

'Glittery dust,' Crispy said, pointing at Fran, whose legs were bulging in her jumpsuit, little trails of glitter falling from her ankles.

Flappy spiralled down, landing with a thud on top of Tiny Fists.

THE CROWD WENT WILD!

Fran punched the air in triumph.

'PEANUT WINS!' Crispy cried. 'But will the evil duo be back in episode two?'

The crowd erupted into whoops and cheers and leapt to their feet – Fran bowed to the standing ovation in front of her, then turned and flew fast towards Crispy.

'Peanut?' she spat. 'Seriously. PEANUT?!'

'PEA-NUT! PEA-NUT! PEA-NUT!' the crowd chanted.

'It's stuck now,' Crispy said with a smirk.

'Well, maybe Peanut could have a name change to Superior Being of Fabulousness or something?' Fran suggested. 'Oh, I know! Fairy God.'

'No,' Patricia the producer said firmly. 'You can't change your character name now, Fran. In *Fairy Fightz* you play the role of Peanut.'

'Can I have your tiny autograph, Peanut?' a witch squealed in Fran's face.

The fabulous fairy turned to Crispy, a black look in her eyes. 'I will get my revenge, Crispy.'

'Take the pen and sign the paper, Peanut,' Crispy said mockingly, as Fran grabbed the huge witch-sized pen with both hands. It was too heavy and slipped right through her arms, hitting the floor with a *clang*.

'I'm going home,' Fran said, her beehive flopping. 'Peanut OUT.'

RITZY CITY POST

EXCLUSIVE INTERVIEW WITH FRAN, THE *FAIRY FIGHTZ* STAR WHO PLAYS THE ROLE OF PEANUT!

Reporter: Are you actually … a peanut?

Fran: PARDON?

Reporter: You smell a bit like a peanut. And your face looks a bit like –

Fran: MY FACE LOOKS FABULOUS AND NOT AT ALL PEANUT-LIKE.

Reporter: What inspired you to call your character Peanut?

Fran: Crispy named me.

Reporter: Oh, we should interview Crispy then.

Fran: But –

Reporter: Crispy, why were you inspired to call Fran's character Peanut?

Crispy: Because she is actually a peanut.
Fran: I'M A FAIRY!
Crispy: A peanut that thinks it's a fairy.
Reporter: Fascinating.

BOOM

Tiga squinted as she stepped into the flames to tell her story. She was the last one. The Points had been impressed and terrified by Fluffanora's tale of the killer cat that could slide through keyholes. Even Idabelle had shivered.

'Um, I don't know many spooky stories,' Tiga began. 'But there is one. In a dark forest, just like this one, but above the pipes, there was a ghost. They say she roamed the forest in perfect circles looking for living people who she would guide to a deep, dark well. She kept them there for ever, and with every one she collected, she came a little bit more back to life.'

'TIGA!' Fran cheered, waving from a leaf on a nearby tree.

'Wait,' Idabelle said, glancing around. 'How did you get in?'

'Oh, you thought you did a secret meeting spell, did you?' Fran said, rolling her eyes. She flew up to them and landed on a little rock next to Fluffanora, leaning back like she was lazing on a sun lounger. 'Those spells don't work on fairies. Our eyeballs can see right through them.'

'I knew Crispy saw me earlier,' Tiga said. 'She looked straight at me.'

'You know,' Fran continued, 'that's why I'm trying to convince Peggy to let us fairies be the police force in Ritzy City. We could be called THE FABULOUS FORCE! And we could use the outfits we wear for *Fairy Fightz*.' She pulled at her jumpsuit, making it stretch and ping back into place. 'They are stretchy and good for crime fighting.'

Idabelle groaned.

'So what are we doing?' Fran asked.

'This is a Points meeting,' Catriona Catcat said, pointedly. 'You can't be here.'

'We're telling spooky stories,' Tiga said.

'*Oh*,' Fran said with a smirk, rubbing her tiny hands together. 'I have a spooky story.'

'SHE'S NOT ALLOWED!' Francesca Fignettle shouted. 'WE DIDN'T INVITE HER. AND HER WINGS ARE HITTING MY SPIRIT MOUSE RIGHT IN THE NOSE!'

Idabelle pinched the bridge of her nose. 'She can tell her little story.'

'It's quite big, actually,' Fran said, puffing out her chest. 'It's about a terrifying group of flying monsters. One has a melted-looking face and the other has jumbo wings.'

'Those are your friends,' Melodie McDamp said. 'Crispy and Julie Jumbo Wings.'

'Crispy and Julie Jumbo Wings are *not* my friends,' Fran scoffed. 'I just spend all my time with them because ...' She trailed off and pretended to spot something interesting in the trees.

'There is nothing spooky about your little fairy friends,' Bertha Bram said, holding the remaining jam stars as far away from Fran as possible. 'These snacks are for *invited* witches only. You weren't invited, and you're not a witch.'

'She'll have to leave before the next bit,' Melodie McDamp whispered to Idabelle. Tiga heard every word clearly and watched as Fran's beehive tilted to the side, which was what it did when she was listening.

'Well I'll be off,' Fran said, shooting Tiga a knowing look. Then much to Tiga's surprise, she shot through a bush, out towards the fairy caravan park.

'That's not like Fran,' Tiga said quietly.

Fluffanora looked at her watch. It had two witches on it – one tall, one short – as the hands, and the numbers were twelve different types of shoe. 'Just look at the time! It's a short witch past the slippers, Tiga, so we should be off.'

'Wait,' Idabelle said. 'For the finale of all our meetings, we try an ancient dead spell.'

‘Why?’ Fluffanora said with a shiver. ‘Ancient spells are out of date and dangerous. They’ve expired. They’re dead.’

Idabelle cackled and grabbed a jam star, squishing it in her fist before lobbing it on to the fire.

‘That’s what they *tell* you, but no spell really expires. It just becomes old and twisted. But twisted spells can be fun!’

‘I think we should go, Tiga,’ Fluffanora said, with a hint of panic in her voice that Tiga had never heard before. They both stood up, but Idabelle flicked her finger and shoved them back down on their seats.

‘Do you know who started the Points?’ Idabelle asked Tiga.

Tiga shook her head helplessly. She glanced at Fluffanora, who was trying to lift herself off the stone. She was struggling, like her body and the stone were one and the same thing.

‘The Ritzy Six,’ Idabelle rasped. ‘A mysterious group of witches who lived a long time ago. Each of the six had a special power, and they caused glorious havoc in Ritzy City. Then one day, the Ritzy Six were caught and trapped somewhere, but only a few good witches knew where. However, before they were captured, they hid their magic at the very top of Pearl Peak, in a sealed house that no one but them could enter, ready for their return. And so the question remains: where are the Ritzy Six? It's Sinkville's biggest secret.'

Tiga breathed a sigh of relief. Thank goodness they were trapped somewhere. She'd been half expecting Idabelle to reveal they were hiding in the trees around them!

Idabelle whipped out a jam jar. 'This is where the Ritzy Six are hidden!'

Tiga let out a surprised scream, causing Bertha Bram to drop the plate of jam stars.

'It took ages to figure it out,' Idabelle said proudly. 'But I found an old *Ritzy City Post* interview with Mavis who owns the jam stall. She was the one who suggested a jam jar to trap the Ritzy Six, *and* she volunteered to look after

it. Once I knew that, I got Melodie to distract the old fool by pretending to be interested in her jam jars shaped like cats. I sneaked behind her jam stall and I GOT IT.'

'That makes Mavis Sinkville's biggest hero,' Tiga said. 'Well, until she let the jam jar fall into your hands.'

'This has all got really weird,' Fluffanora said, sweating slightly as she tried in vain to pull herself off her stone stool. She stopped and tapped her watch. 'And now it's five tall ladies past the slipper. It's practically one short lady on the boot, so really we'd better be going.'

Idabelle smirked and began to slowly twist the jam jar lid.

'For years, the Points have tried to track down the Ritzy Six. Our heroes! The very reason we sit here around this fire today. They can teach us to be more powerful than any other witches in the world! They can get to the magic at the top of the mountain! And now all I have to do to bring them back is use an old, expired spell.'

'Which one?' Fluffanora demanded.

'The Green Blood – you say the spell with the names

of the witches you want to bring back, while in the presence of *green blood*. It only expired because no witch could work out the green blood bit. But I realised, Tiga is green – green because she's a new witch in Sinkville, plus her real surname is Green, so we've got all bases covered. No one is more of a green blood witch than Tiga!'

Tiga's stomach flip-flopped.

'Why am I here then?' Fluffanora spat furiously.

'Well, Tiga can never do things on her own, according to my sister, so we had to invite one of her friends. But which witch to choose!'

The Points cackled madly.

'We couldn't have Peggy Pigwiggle,' Idabelle said with a snigger. 'She's the Top Witch and the Top Witch could never come to something like this. Lizzy Beast would only break something – or us!'

They cackled some more.

'Felicity would have figured out something was up. Aggie Hoof is the most irritating witch alive. You never seem to see the twins Milly and Molly any more, and to be honest, I completely forgot about the other one,' she said, clicking her fingers while searching for the name.

'Patty Pigeon,' Tiga said quietly.

'PATTY PIGEON, OF COURSE!' Idabelle said, making the others dissolve into cackles once more. 'That just left you, Fluffanora. Brave, stubborn, curious. You were *perfect*. Tiga would never have come here without you saying it was a good idea.'

Fluffanora scowled as Idabelle threw the jam jar lid on the fire. Melodie blew a bored bubble as the others clasped their hands excitedly.

'If we can bring back the Ritzy Six, the Points will be unstoppable! We'll be able to do anything we want,' Idabelle roared.

'Can I buy more spirit animals?' Francesca Fignettle oozed, but Idabelle was in a giddy trance.

Melodie McDamp blew another bubble and popped it with her finger. 'I'm going to keep my job at the Mermaid Museum. I like the work, and the uniform.'

Idabelle's eyes were wide and fixed on the jam jar as

she held it up. With a swift flick of the finger she sent Tiga somersaulting upwards and held her suspended above the flames.

'PUT ME DOWN!' Tiga cried.

'Six original Points, one jam jar,' Idabelle Bat hissed.

'NO!' Tiga and Fluffanora shouted in unison.

Idabelle smirked and launched the jam jar into the air.

'Burn you back to who you are.'

It tumbled past Tiga's nose and towards the fire. Tiga tried to grab it, but it was no good. Everything seemed like it was moving in slow motion. The Points were rising to their feet. Fluffanora's mouth was sagging into a gloomy frown. Francesca Fignettle was ranting something about a spirit butterfly, but it came in long drowned-out groans and Tiga filtered it out.

Then came the buzz. The shot of glitter! The –

'Fran!' Tiga cried, as Fran crashed into the jam jar. She balanced on the edge of the rim as it spun around and around, trying to get a grip, but she flipped backwards, her sparkly jumpsuit ripping as she went.

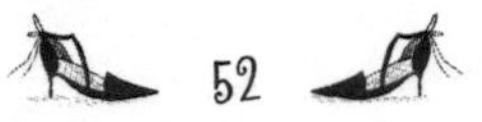

Fran slipped into the jam. It landed with a hiss in the fire.

'Fran!' Tiga cried, racing over to fish the fairy out.

There was an explosion of black smoke, followed by a strange squealing sound, as six pointy hats leapt from the flames with an assortment of witches attached to them. They were wearing twigs and leaves, fashioned into dresses.

The cackling was unbearable.

'We did it!' Idabelle squealed, waving her hands madly and completely losing her composure for a second. She coughed and straightened herself up. Her eyes filled with delighted tears. 'THEY'RE BACK.'

'Well, you've made a *real mess*,' Fluffanora said, shaking her head. 'And if they think they're going to get clothes from Brew's to replace the twig-and-leaf dresses then YOU ARE SADLY MISTAKEN.'

Idabelle stalked over and stretched out a hand. 'I'm Idabelle, head of the Points.'

Six, the tallest of the Ritzy Six, stepped forward

and grinned. 'Thank you, Points witch, but we are the leaders now.' She turned towards Pearl Peak. 'We must go home and get our magic.'

'No!' Idabelle demanded. 'First you teach us your special powers and then we wreak havoc!'

'Patience, little witch,' said Five. 'All the things we need are at the top of Pearl Peak.'

And off they ran.

'WAIT FOR MEEEEEE!' Idabelle cried, as the younger Points raced after the Ritzy Six. The fire went out with a pop, leaving Tiga, Fluffanora and Fran alone in the darkness.

'Fran,' Tiga whispered, fishing the jam jar out of the ashes and scooping Fran out from inside it. The tiny fairy coughed up an even tinier puff of smoke.

'I remember the Ritzy Six,' she said. 'Bad, bad, ba–'

She fainted in Tiga's palm.

Tiga placed Fran gently on the forest floor and leaned down to check she was breathing.

Fluffanora flicked her finger and mumbled. 'Back you

go, one, two, three, in time you'll still remember me.'

Tiga looked at her, an eyebrow raised.

'Rewind spell. She won't remember the last three hours or so. Oh, stop looking at me like that, Tiga! You know we'll have to fix this, and Fran would only try to stop us, or at the very least, get in the way. Or she'd do a newspaper interview and tell them about the Ritzy Six, and then the whole town would panic. No, we have to sort this. Before anyone finds out.'

Fluffanora was right. Tiga reluctantly flicked her finger and Fran's limp body went flying off through the forest.

'I did a finger flick to put her back in her caravan,' Tiga said. 'She'll be tucked up in bed when she wakes.'

Fluffanora raised an eyebrow. 'Are you sure …? You're not … *great* at that spell.'

'Positive,' Tiga said with a nod.

'Right.' Fluffanora looked unconvinced. 'Well, we need to tell Felicity. She'll be able to help. Oh, I hate it when she's right.' She grabbed Tiga's arm and dragged her back out of the forest.

A REVIEW OF *FAIRY FIGHTZ*

The latest TV sensation to hit our spoons has witches all over Sinkville going crazy for *Fairy Fightz*! The cast consists of three key members. Patricia the producer thinks more characters could be added if the show proves successful. Fan favourite Peanut is played by the fabulous Fran. Peanut wears a sparkly jumpsuit and drops glittery dust out of her trousers like a pro. She dominated in episode one, but Patricia the producer has hinted that things might not always be so rosy for the fairy star.

Her arch-rivals are the terrifyingly named Flappy, and her sidekick Tiny Fists. Tiny Fists wears the best headgear in the show, though did no flying and had very few

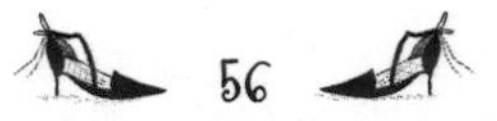

choreographed moves. She seems to rely on Flappy, whose wings are huge and whose moves are impressive.

We sat down with Patricia in her plastic castle office in Brollywood and asked her some questions.

Reporter: Who is your favourite character?
Patricia the producer: Peanut.
Reporter: Why?
Patricia the producer: Because if I said anyone other than Fran's character, she'd throw a strop and put the whole TV show at risk of being shut down. Her last strop involved her protesting outside the shop that sells pictures of famous Brollywood faces. She spotted they weren't all of her and chained herself to the door, so no one could get in. She shouted 'MY

FACE OR NOTHING!' for three whole days. I can still hear it echoing in my head.

Reporter: What will happen to *Cooking for Tiny People* while Fran is filming *Fairy Fightz*?

Patricia the producer: We thought about asking Crispy to stand in for her, but Crispy has taken over directing *Fairy Fightz* and is doing a wonderful job. Plus Fran threw a melon at me when I suggested Crispy could take over. There will be no new *Cooking for Tiny People* while Fran is filming *Fairy Fightz*, but ... her new cookbook, *Cooking for Tiny People: The Complete Microscopic Collection*, will be available in all good Sinkville bookshops in the meantime.

Reporter: And one more question. I've always wondered ... why is your office a big plastic castle?

Patricia the producer: We filmed a TV show a long time ago, when Fran was a young star. We called it *Microscopic Princess in a Big Plastic Castle*. People liked our twist on princesses – she was a fairy-sized architect. The series ended when Fran demanded we change the castle material from plastic to gold. We just don't have those kind of budgets.

Reporter: And one more question. What's your greatest achievement in your role as Patricia the producer, so far?

Patricia the producer: Dealing with Fran after she won the award for Best and Only Fairy Film of the Year. She demanded that we train a cat to transport her to the set in the morning. But all cats hate her and I couldn't find one willing to do it.

Cats

Tiga and Fluffanora raced back to Linden House and didn't stop until they reached the door. Tiga gripped the handle tightly and panted, as Fluffanora collapsed in a heap.

The door creaked open.

'What's happened now?' Felicity Bat groaned.

'Why did you go?' Felicity Bat spat. '*WHY?*'

'Curiosity?' Fluffanora said.

'And before you say it, Felicity, we *know* – curiosity killed the cat,' Tiga added.

There was a hissing sound and then a sharp crack as

a large clump of cats fell through the ceiling and landed at Tiga's feet. They looked up at her.

'Why are there cats falling through the roof?' Tiga asked.

One of them licked her boot.

'You just did a spell,' Felicity Bat said impatiently.

'What, "curiosity killed the cat"?!' Tiga cried as another clump of cats fell on her. 'That's just a saying. People above the pipes say it all the time.'

'Well down here,' Felicity Bat said, 'it's a spell.'

Fluffanora leaned closer to Tiga. 'It saves unwanted cats. You know, strays and things. If you want to help some cats, you say it.'

'THAT DOESN'T MAKE ANY SENSE!' Tiga cried.

'Well, what do you expect from a Catcat family spell?' Felicity Bat said. 'Did Catriona not tell you about it at the Points gathering? She's always boasting about her family's spells.'

'She didn't go into detail, although Idabelle

mentioned the one about turning witches into cats … just not the … ceiling cat one,' Tiga said.

Felicity put her head in her hands and let out a muffled scream.

'I think she finds us frustrating,' Fluffanora said with a smile.

Felicity Bat went black in the eyes and flew towards Tiga. 'I find *her* frustrating,' she seethed, prodding Tiga with her finger. 'She barely knows any spells. She doesn't take my warnings about my sister seriously. SHE ALWAYS CAUSES TROUBLE.'

'*I* barely know any spells either,' Fluffanora said, flicking her finger and making a notebook appear. It had *FLUFFANORA'S SPELL LIST* written in perfect green ink on the front. She flicked through and looked up. 'But I did know that curiosity killed the –'

'DON'T SAY IT!' Felicity Bat screamed.

Fluffanora closed her notebook slowly and tucked it into her pocket.

'She's right,' Tiga said, slumping on the sofa. 'I hardly

know any spells. I don't even write the ones I do know in a notebook. They'd barely fill a page!'

'You're good at being my best friend, though!' Peggy said as she came cantering into the room and halted in the middle of them. 'Wait … why so serious? What did I miss? And whose are these cats?' She lowered her voice to a whisper. 'Or are they here to complain about something?'

'Tiga's messed everything up again,' Felicity Bat said as she floated slowly towards the door. 'I have my own problems to deal with, I can't spend my life sorting out yours.'

'But the cats?' Peggy pressed. 'Why the cats?'

'Tiga did a spell,' Felicity Bat said faintly. 'And this time I'm not helping them – THEY ARE ON THEIR OWN.'

'Technically we're far from alone,' Fluffanora said, lifting up two of the cats.

Felicity Bat rolled her eyes as she floated out of the room, and with the flick of a finger, slammed the door.

'NO!' Tiga cried. 'We didn't even get to tell her about the return of the Ritzy Six.'

'She's too angry, Tiga. We'll have to fix this one ourselves,' Fluffanora said.

Peggy's mouth was hanging open and the cat in her arms was licking her glasses. 'The Ritzy Six? Not *the* Ritzy Six?'

Tiga nodded gravely. 'I tried to tell Felicity, but she was furious we'd even gone to the Points meeting, and then the cats fell from the ceiling and, well ...'

'I've read about the Ritzy Six,' Peggy said.

'Well, you'll probably get to meet them soon,' Fluffanora said. 'Idabelle brought them back – at the Points meeting. We saw it all.'

Peggy scooped up a cat and held it tightly. 'Did they say anything when they came back? Maybe they're nice now?'

'I don't think they are,' Tiga said. 'They raced off to Pearl Peak – they said everything they needed to be all powerful and wreak havoc was there.'

'I remember,' Peggy said, pacing the room. 'The Ritzy Six locked their powerful magic in their home before they were caught. The only way to stop them is to get there before them.'

'Oh!' Tiga said, breathing a sigh of relief. 'Well, that's not impossible, is it? We can stop them! I mean, I can see Pearl Peak from the window here. It's just a mountain. I'm really good at climbing. We can get to the top in no time. Let's go!'

Fluffanora grabbed the side of the sofa to steady herself.

'You can't just climb Pearl Peak, Tiga,' Peggy said. 'It might look like a spindly mountain, but it's a whole other world, with its own rules.'

Peggy clapped her hands and a black sled landed with a thud in the middle of the room.

'What are we supposed to do with that?' Fluffanora asked.

'Well, there's snow up there,' Peggy replied, herding the cats and attaching them to the sled in neat rows. 'So you might need a cat-drawn sled.'

'Thanks,' Tiga said with a gulp as she watched the mist swirl around the tip of Pearl Peak. 'We need all the help we can get.'

'And I'm coming too,' Peggy said, nestling into the sled and grabbing the reins. The cats arched their backs, ready to run. 'Because the sled is mine, the cats will only respond if I'm driving.'

'And three is better,' Fluffanora said in a whisper as she eyed the mountain. 'The more of us that go up, the more likely it is that one of us will reach the top …'

To Pearl Peak!

'Pearl Peak *proper*?' came Mavis's voice from behind her jam stall. 'I know a bit about it, yes. There's Pearl Peak New Town, where Aggie Hoof and Felicity Bat live. And then you have Pearl Peak *Old* Town. That part is in the mountain, where the most evil witches lived. No one's been there in years! I believe it's magic-protected. You'd be mad to go. MAD!' She popped up from behind the stall and spotted Peggy crouched in the cat sled, with Tiga and Fluffanora trying to assemble the cats in a neat row.

Peggy smiled meekly.

'OH NO!' Mavis shouted, throwing her hands in the air and toppling her perfect pyramid of jam jars. Tiga

sidestepped as they smashed at her feet. 'The sled … YOU'RE NOT GOING *UP* PEARL PEAK, ARE YOU?'

Peggy blinked and swallowed awkwardly. 'Maybe.'

'We need to fix a … um … thing,' Tiga said. She didn't want to tell Mavis anything. If she noticed her not-so-carefully-guarded Ritzy Six jam jar was missing, then she'd alert everyone and the whole town would panic.

Mavis clutched her heart. 'I can't let you go alone.' She tried to step out from behind the stall but got her legs tangled and landed at Fluffanora's feet in a neat little knot.

Fluffanora picked a pot of jam off the stall and scooped out a big spoonful. 'Something makes me think we'd be better off without you, Mavis. But we could do with some of your delicious jam to keep us going.'

Mavis sprang to her feet and began loading jar after jar into the cart. 'TAKE IT ALL! OH, IF IT'LL HELP, TAKE IT ALL!'

☆☆☆

When they got to Pearl Peak, witches in their black mansions peeked out of the windows, watching their every move.

'What *are* they staring at?' Fluffanora scoffed as she scooped out a big handful of jam and shoved it in her mouth.

'CHAAAAAAAARGE!' Peggy cried as the cats reluctantly slinked forward.

Tiga looked from Peggy to Fluffanora and back again.

'I suppose it's not every day they see the Top Witch riding a sled pulled by snail-paced cats and bellowing CHARGE.'

'CHAAAAARGE!' Peggy cried optimistically, again. One of the cats sat down and started licking its tail.

'We'll get to the top in no time,' Peggy said brightly as the snow began to fall. Fluffanora flicked her finger and a huge cape with fur trim wrapped itself around Tiga.

Fluffanora's outfit had morphed completely. Now she wore a stylish mix of bright yellow snow trousers featuring cat-shaped pockets, teamed with a slouchy jumper embroidered with a glistening F. She'd topped it all off with a glittery cropped coat. She looked down and inspected her feet, which she'd clad in huge chunky boots with glitter laces to match her jacket. She flicked her finger once more and some icicle earrings flew past Tiga's nose and hooked themselves on to Fluffanora's ears.

'I don't know how you throw together cool outfits like that,' Tiga said.

Fluffanora flicked her finger and a fur trim burst from Peggy's hat.

'Much warmer!' Peggy said, doing the thumbs up.

'It's a skill,' Fluffanora said with a smile. 'I'm thinking of selling my special dressing spells. I just need to find a way of programming each spell so it would know what was in the user's wardrobe.'

‘I bet Felicity Bat could help,’ Peggy said.

Fluffanora’s smile faded. ‘I doubt she’ll ever speak to us again after we went to the Points meeting.’

‘I’m sure she’ll forgive us. If we fix all this,’ Tiga said.

‘Unlikely,’ Fluffanora said. ‘That witch could hold a grudge for ever. She’s the granddaughter of Celia Crayfish.’

Tiga laughed. ‘Did she hold a lot of grudges too?’

Fluffanora, Peggy and the sled cats came to an abrupt halt.

‘No, Tiga,’ Fluffanora said. ‘She actually *invented* grudges.’

‘Oh,’ Tiga said quietly as they carried on through the thickening snow.

‘Do you think they’ll be easy to spot?’ Peggy asked.

‘They’re wearing twigs and leaves on a snowy mountain,’ Fluffanora said. ‘So yes, I’d bet all my jam on it.’

FAIRY FIGHTZ INTERVIEW WITH FLAPPY!

Reporter: Flappy, your real name is Julie Jumbo Wings – why didn't you keep that for your *Fairy Fightz* character?

Julie Jumbo Wings: It's JUST JULIE!

Reporter: OK … Tell us a bit about your character.

Julie Jumbo Wings: Flappy is the evil villain, and is terrifying. She likes flower arranging, naps and joy.

Reporter: She doesn't sound very terrifying.

Julie Jumbo Wings: Flappy is HORRIFIC.

Aggie Hoof Hears Things

Aggie Hoof skipped along the Linden House corridor to Felicity Bat's door and readied her hand to knock. But she stopped when she heard a voice and pressed her ear to the door.

'We'll get you back up the pipes in no time. I just need to find the right one, or you could end up somewhere strange. Luckily you're rare, so that narrows it down.'

Aggie Hoof's eyes widened. 'Fel-Fel has another *friend*?' She turned the handle on the door and leapt inside.

'Ah ha!' she shouted.

'What?' Felicity Bat said, looking up from her book.

'Who were you talking to?' Aggie Hoof asked.

'No one,' Felicity Bat said dismissively.

'Then my ears are hearing things again,' Aggie Hoof said, jumping up on to the bed.

She didn't notice Felicity Bat's boot on the floor, wiggling all by itself.

Mean Lock

Tiga stared up at the gigantic mountain and then at the large black iron gates guarding the path that led inside.

'What *exactly* is inside?' she whispered, but Fluffanora was too busy rattling the gates to notice.

'It's locked,' she said.

'I know what to do,' Peggy said. She took a deep breath, raised the reins high, then cracked them back down. The cats went flying. They shot straight through the gaps in the gate, but the sled was too big! It hit the metal bars and flipped up, sending Peggy crunching into the bars. Only her nose got through.

'Nope,' she said, peeling herself off the gate and

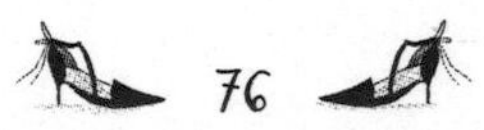

pulling the cats back through. 'We'll have to find another way in.'

Fluffanora flicked her finger and the gates began to wobble and smoke. But they didn't open.

'Do you think it's a challenge?' she asked Peggy. 'Aren't there supposed to be challenges?'

'What exactly is inside the mountain?' Tiga asked again, but they weren't listening.

'We could try a potion?' Peggy suggested. 'Something with snow?'

'WHAT EXACTLY IS IN THE MOUNTAIN?' Tiga bellowed. 'WILL SOMEONE *PLEASE* ANSWER ME!'

The gates creaked open.

'Ah!' Fluffanora said, shaking the snow off her gloves and stepping through the gates. 'It was a Mean Lock.'

'What's that?' Tiga asked.

'It only opens for mean people,' Peggy said as she and the sled slid on through. 'You shouted so aggressively, the gates thought you were mean.'

'Gates can't *think*,' Tiga said.

Fluffanora and Peggy chuckled.

'Everything can think with a little magic,' Fluffanora said. 'Now come on, we need to at least get to the second level as quickly as possible before nightfall. They say strange creatures roam the mountain at night – the higher up we are, the less likely we are to want to run back.'

Tiga shivered and looked around her. The place was dark and frozen – an icy cave with carefully carved paths that splintered and scuttled in all directions. Above her head was a frozen ceiling, blocking her view overhead.

Tiga gulped, just as BROOMSTICK BOOM, the popular witch board game, landed at their feet.

'Broomstick Boom!' Tiga cried, opening the box.

But it wasn't Broomstick Boom inside. It was another game entirely – this one looked old and was made of cold black stone and ice.

'I don't know if you should touch it,' Peggy said, her voice shaking.

Fluffanora shushed her. 'It's obviously part of the mountain's game. Go on, Tiga.'

'The mountain plays a game?' Tiga said as she flipped the latch on the old stone game. It creaked open like the door to a haunted house.

'It's just a board,' she said, holding it close to her nose to inspect it.

The path on the board curled around the inside of a spindly mountain. And there were three player pieces – one, a witch in a sparkly hat, another witch that glowed a luminous green, and a third that had a cart with a bunch of cats pulling it.

'It's us, but how did it know?' Fluffanora said, looking around her. 'The sparkly one is me, Peggy is the one with the cart and cats, and you're the green one – because you're Tiga Green, and the green blood thing. But how would the game know that?'

'And what's that little light further up the mountain?' Peggy asked, rubbing the game with her finger, as if trying to rub the light out. 'It's not a smudge.'

Tiga moved them to the tip of the mountain and closed her eyes, hoping it would magically transport them there. But when she opened her eyes again, the pieces were sliding all the way back to the beginning.

Not far from the start point, scratched into the game, was a picture of three broomsticks and a large hole.

'I don't like the look of that,' Tiga whispered, as Fluffanora slowly raised her arm and pointed at three objects glowing in the distance.

'Broomsticks,' Peggy said. 'Do you think we have to ride them?'

Pop!

'Did you hear that?' Tiga whispered. 'It sounded like –'

'Melodie McDamp blowing a bubble,' Fluffanora groaned, taking a wary step backwards. 'They got through the gate too. That must be what that little light on the game is – the other players.'

Tiga looked up.

'Stay hidden,' Fluffanora whispered, pulling them all

to the side. 'They can't see us – they'll know we're trying to get to the Ritzy Six.'

The ice above her head shook slightly and Tiga could just make out boots, though the ice was so thick she thought she might be seeing things.

Then a face smooshed against the ice!

The three of them slid back into the shadows.

'What if she sees us – or the cats?' Peggy whispered.

Tiga held a finger to her lips.

The boots above them tottered on and disappeared.

'How did they get up there? That means they're ahead,' Tiga said glumly. 'And the Ritzy Six are ahead of them. How are we ever going to reach the Points with Idabelle and her friends between us?'

'All we can do is try,' Fluffanora said as she tiptoed up to the brooms and grabbed one of them. 'Are you comin–'

But the broom was off – spiralling down into a deep dark hole.

'Fluffanora!' Peggy cried. She turned to the cats.

'Right, you all need to get on the sled, which I will balance on my head, while riding the broom.'

The cats looked appropriately concerned.

'Are those … houses down there?' Tiga asked as she squinted into the frosty hole.

Peggy nodded. 'They call it Under Peak. The place where witches live deep underground. We must have to go down to go up to the next level …'

'I don't suppose the witches down there are friendly, are they?' Tiga asked.

Peggy cackled, then stopped when she realised Tiga wasn't joking. 'Oh no, Tiga. They're the *worst*. The good thing is there are only a few of them.'

Tiga shakily held on to the broom and it dragged her over the edge and into the darkness below.

The Points Take the Lead

Idabelle Bat sniffed the air. It smelled of that familiar Pearl Peak frostiness, but with a hint of Tiga.

'You don't think they got past the gates, do you?' Melodie McDamp said, as if reading Idabelle's mind. 'Because they might try to ruin our plans. They could put the Ritzy Six back in the jam jar!'

Idabelle rolled the possibilities around in her brain for a second and then shook her head as if shaking the silly thoughts out again.

'Don't be ridiculous, Melodie,' she spat. 'They aren't mean. They'd never get past the gates.'

She took out a stone game just like the one Tiga had found. Their board had four pieces – a witch holding a bat, a witch blowing a mermaid-scale bubble, a witch holding a tray of treats, and a witch with a cat-ear headband. But just below their pieces, a little further down the mountain there was a small light.

'What do you suppose that light is?' Catriona Catcat said, rubbing it. 'A smudge? A glitch?'

'I don't know, but it can't be Tiga,' Idabelle said. 'It's impossible. Now come on, we need to catch up with the Ritzy Six! I want to learn their secrets – I want to be the most powerful witch in Sinkville!'

'I think Tiga *did* get past the gate!' Bertha Bram cheered.

'Don't be ridiculous,' Idabelle hissed, flicking her finger and sending Bertha Bram flying. She stomped ahead, up a winding path that disappeared into the mist. 'Level two, here we come.'

'Did you hear that whispering noise?' Bertha Bram said, grabbing on to Melodie's arm.

Melodie blew a bubble. 'Uh-huh, it sounded like a ghost.'

'Don't ghosts sound just like us?' Bertha Bram whimpered.

'Yeah, but their words are invisible,' Catriona Catcat said as she scuttled after Idabelle.

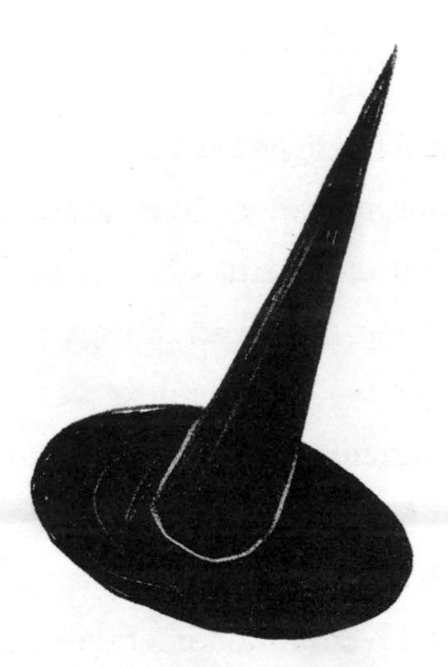

The Missing Peanut

Outside the *Fairy Fightz* set, the crowds were swarming – some in glittery jumpsuits, others wearing fake wings and caps that said things like 'Punchin' Peanut' and 'Flappy For Ever'.

It was almost time for the next part of *Fairy Fightz*, but no one could find the star.

'FRAAAAAAAN!' came the tiny cries of a worried Crispy. 'FRAAAAAAAN!'

'She's probably hiding for attention,' Julie Jumbo Wings said. 'She'll surprise us when we start filming. She'll explode out of a rainbow or something.'

Crispy smooshed her face up against Fran's caravan window. 'No, this isn't like her. She always wants to be in

complete control. She'd never let me direct all by myself. I think I went too far, calling her Peanut.'

Crispy drooped in the air a little.

'But she *did* say she'd get revenge on me, so maybe this is all part of her plan.'

Julie Jumbo Wings nodded. 'That would be more like Fran.'

'I'm going in,' Crispy said, tentatively reaching for the handle.

'SHE'S GOING TO AMBUSH US!' Julie Jumbo Wings cried, shooting off into the trees, leaving Crispy alone.

Crispy raised her fists as she entered. 'Fran, you will not smack me with your beehive again.'

The caravan was empty.

'Fran?' Crispy whispered, just as there was an almighty bang and the fabulous fairy tumbled out of one of the kitchen cupboards.

'*Why* were you in the *cupboard*?' Crispy asked.

Fran's beehive looked like woodland creatures had

tried to comb it. Her sparkly jumpsuit was burnt around the edges and her lipstick was smudged into a red moustache.

'What happened? You need to go on stage for *Fairy Fightz* in a few minutes! The crowd is already cheering for you!'

Chants of 'PEA-NUT!' echoed around them.

'The WHOLE TOWN is chanting for you, Fran. Well, say something!'

Fran fixed her beehive and stared at Crispy as if she were mad. 'What are you *talking about*, Crispy? They're chanting about a peanut. I'm *Fran.* And apparently, I decided to sleep in my cupboard … because … Well, I can't remember that bit.'

'Don't care,' Crispy said, grabbing Fran by the arm. 'We need to go *now*, or Patricia will cancel *Fairy Fightz*. And we can't have it cancelled, the whole town LOVED part one.'

Fran laughed. 'I don't know what little game this is, but we haven't filmed that yet, Crispy! We finished

rehearsals … and then I ended up here in a slightly burnt outfit, which I cannot explain, but I actually think it looks fabulous – because it's adorning *me*.'

Patricia the producer came flying over with her umbrella and peered inside the caravan. She fell to the ground with a thud when she saw Fran.

'OH, HOW WONDERFUL! Excellent make-up and I like the slightly burnt look of the outfit. Oh, how dramatic! Everyone is going to love it, Peanut, you star.'

'*WHY* are you calling me Peanut?!' Fran cried, but Patricia the producer had zoomed off.

Crispy flew over and knocked on Fran's beehive. 'Hello?'

'Have you lost your mind, Crispy?'

'Have *you*?' Crispy asked. 'Did you leave the last three hours in that cupboard?'

Fran rolled her eyes. 'Crispy, I will not have you trying to confuse an expert actress with this silly nonsense. Now,' she said, rising into the air. 'LET'S GO FILM *FAIRY FIGHTZ* PART ONE!'

Fran Does Part One, Again

Crispy smacked her hand to her head.

'Why is Fran doing the lines and moves from part *one*?' Patricia the producer demanded.

Julie and Donna, or Flappy and Tiny Fists as they were known to the fans, scuttled along the edge of the stage.

'What is Fran doing?' Julie Jumbo Wings asked loudly.

'PEA-NUT! PEA-NUT! PEA-NUT!' the crowd chanted.

Fran stopped and stared at them. '*WHO?*' She turned to Crispy. 'Why are they all dressed like that? Did you leak Fluffanora's outfit designs? I told you, no one should see the outfits until the first episode!'

Flappy launched into action, as planned, grabbing Tiny Fists and hurtling her through the air towards Peanut.

'Ha! Peanut, your good days are OVER!' she cried.

Fran turned slowly. 'I don't understand why everyone seems to be calling me Pea–'

SMACK!

'She was meant to duck!' Flappy said as the crowd booed. 'Crispy, what's wrong with her?'

Fran marched across the stage and grabbed Julie by a jumbo wing. 'Flappy,' she said sternly. 'That was not in the script.'

'Yes it was, we practised part two four times earlier and you said, "I DON'T KNOW WHY WE'RE PRACTISING, I'M *PERFECT*."'

Fran tapped her chin. 'That does sound like me, but this is part *one* … You are being incredibly unprofessional.'

'Stop having a conversation in the middle of the show,' Crispy pleaded. 'Go to page three of the script.'

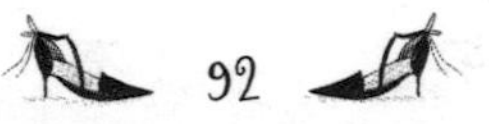

Julie Jumbo Wings looked at Fran and whispered, 'This is when you say, PEANUT WILL NOT BE DEFEATED.'

'CAN SOMEONE TELL ME *WHO*,' Fran roared, 'IS PEANUT?!'

16 The Peggy Problem

'I can't see anything,' Tiga said as the broom tipped her off and flew away. Fluffanora tried to stand up next to her and slipped over, landing with a thud on Peggy.

They'd descended into another cave, only one that was a little less icy. It was muddy and empty, apart from a tiny hole in the wall.

'I suppose,' Tiga said, crawling towards the hole, 'it's this way.'

'But it's so small!' Fluffanora cried. 'How do we get in?'

Peggy squinted at the cats in the darkness. 'We could each tie ourselves to a cat and they could lead the way, pulling us thr–'

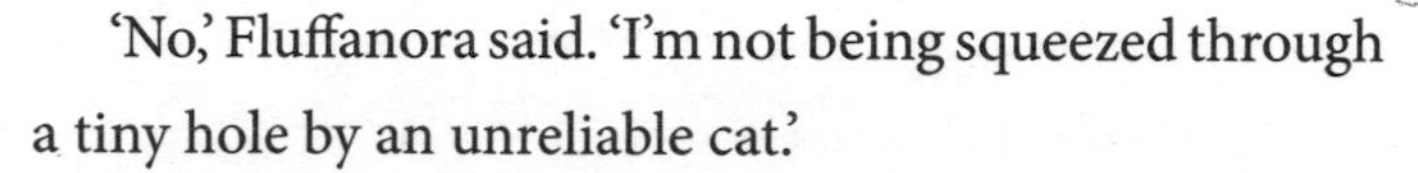

'No,' Fluffanora said. 'I'm not being squeezed through a tiny hole by an unreliable cat.'

The cat looked up at her, quite clearly offended.

'Well, if witches live down here, there must be a way in. It's a test – a trick,' Tiga said, walking towards the hole and smacking off it.

'Did you think it was an illusion?' Peggy said quietly.

'No,' Tiga said, defensively. 'I was just examining it. It's definitely that small.'

Fluffanora got down on her knees. 'I wouldn't be able to crawl through.'

Peggy kneeled down too and reached a hand in. 'Oh! I can feel something squidgy, like a witch's face. And a scarf! And some frazzled hair and –'

She vanished!

'Peggy!' Tiga cried, sticking her head in the hole, which began to grow larger and larger.

'What's happening?' Fluffanora said, sounding furious. 'Where did Peggy go?'

The hole continued to grow larger and larger, letting

out more and more light, until Tiga could see winding streets and witches beyond.

'WELCOME TO THE UNDER PEAK!' a witch with frazzled hair and a large scarf bellowed. Her eyes were gigantic, presumably to see underground. 'Thank you for your payment. You will be refunded if you reach the top.'

'But we didn't make a payment,' Tiga said slowly.

The witch unfurled her scarf and held it up.

Tiga and Fluffanora gasped.

There, embroidered on it like she'd been there for years, was an image of Peggy.

'I'm fine!' the little embroidered image of Peggy said. A tiny embroidered thumbs up appeared next to her. 'You can do this!'

'Peggy?' Tiga cried. She tried to grab the scarf, but the witch yanked it away.

'Did you see the other decoration on her scarf?' Fluffanora whispered. 'A sequin face of Francesca Fignettle. Idabelle must've paid with her, just like we accidentally did with Peggy.'

‘DON’T SCRATCH MY SPIRIT FLY,’ the tiny sequin face said.

‘Now, come on, come on. We don’t often get visitors. It’s only a short walk to the lifts to level two. Just watch out for the helper.’

‘The helper?’ Fluffanora asked, not taking her eyes off the scarf.

‘We’re not going anywhere without our friend,’ Tiga said.

A group of witches rolled past on sparkly boulders, making the ground rumble. The place wasn’t like Peggy had described it at all. There were *hundreds* of witches and shops and lights. It was like a muddier, icier Ritzy City, buried deep inside the mountain.

‘You’ll need these,’ the witch said, ignoring Tiga and handing them some goggles. When Fluffanora tried them on, her eyes tripled in size.

‘I can see everything – it’s so bright!’ she cried.

‘Just watch out for the helper, because a helper is only a help if they are really there for you,’ the witch said

again with a cackle. 'Take Dirt Lane Four, then cross the street at the Mulch Shop – the lifts to the second floor are across from there, next to the toy shop that only sells rocks.'

'We really can't leave without our friend,' Tiga said, falling backwards when she put the goggles on.

'The only way to get your friend off my scarf is to keep going,' the witch said. 'So you'd better get going. I *promise* you will get her back if you reach the top.'

'And we will reach the top,' Fluffanora said. 'We will.'

Tiga thought about it for a moment and then reluctantly took a step forward. 'We'll be back, Peggy!'

'I know!' Peggy said, as she did the thumbs up again. 'I'm doing the thumbs up, can you see?'

'Yes,' Tiga said. 'It appears as a little embroidered thumb next to your face.'

'Excellent!' Peggy said chirpily as if she wasn't stuck on a scarf. 'Oh, and you'll have to take my cats. But they won't move without me holding the reins, so you'll have to carry them.'

Tiga picked up some of the cats and unsuccessfully tried to juggle them as she walked. Fluffanora pulled the sled full of jam and the remaining sleeping cats.

'Dirt Lane One,' Tiga said, reading the signs. Witches on boulders were travelling down the different dirt lanes, jumping off at their destinations. 'Ah,' she said. 'Dirt Lane Four.'

It was the quietest lane. There wasn't a single boulder or witch travelling down it, just the one witch right in the middle.

'Hi!' the witch said. 'I'm Jiggle! And I'm here to help you!'

'What did the witch say about a helper?' Tiga whispered to Fluffanora.

'I can't remember,' Fluffanora whispered back. 'I was too distracted by the fact Peggy has been temporarily turned into an embellishment.'

'Want to play a game?' Jiggle asked. She was a little witch, with mischievous eyes.

'We're already playing a game,' Tiga said, clutching

the stone board game tightly. When she glanced at it, she noticed the Peggy piece was back at the entrance to the Under Peak, whereas she and Fluffanora had moved on. It made her want to go back.

'Oh, come on,' Jiggle said. 'If you win, you get a prize.'

The sides of Dirt Lane Four lit up and a jingle started playing. Jiggle began dancing and miming the words.

'Her name is Jiggle and she's trying to start some fun,
Being great and lovely, like your bestest chum!
She's always being sweet,
Her face is made of meat.
Three cheers for her, yeah, she's Jiggle.'

'Isn't everyone's face *technically* made of meat? That's like saying, "my hair is made of hair" or something,' Fluffanora said.

'I needed something that rhymed with sweet,' Jiggle said.

‘Feet, neat, wheat, beat, pleat?’ Fluffanora said.

Tiga’s eyes widened. ‘I remember what the witch said,’ she whispered urgently. ‘She said, “Watch out for the helper, because a helper is only a help if they are really there for you.” Whatever that means …’

Fluffanora grinned and threw the sled at Jiggle. ‘Here, hold this.’

Their supply of jam jars went flying and smashed and splattered around them, while the sled soared straight through Jiggle and her outstretched arms.

‘JIGGLE!’ she cheered, as she vanished with a *pop*.

‘She’s an incantation,’ Fluffanora said. ‘The way to deal with them is to ask them to hold something – they can’t. When they come into contact with an object it makes them vanish. I was wondering why she added a bit about her face being made of meat. Such an incantation thing to say.’

‘Because she’s made of air and magic,’ Tiga said. ‘I get it. And the witch said a helper is only a help if they are *really there* for you. Jiggle wasn’t really there!’

There was another *pop* and Tiga and Fluffanora found themselves standing next to a toy shop that only sold rocks. The cats and battered sled landed in a neat pile next to them.

'The lifts,' Tiga said, jumping up and down and dropping a bunch of cats. 'We made it! We figured out Jiggle so it must've moved us here – we're one step closer!'

Fluffanora read the plaques on the lifts. There were two lifts, made of glass and standing side by side.

'Tiga, both of them say TO LEVEL TWO.'

'Both of them?' Tiga said. 'Do you think it's a trick?'

'I think everything in this place is a trick,' Fluffanora said.

'So which one is the real lift to level two? How could we possibly know?'

FAIRY FIGHTZ INTERVIEW WITH TINY FISTS!

Reporter: Donna, you play the role of Tiny Fists. What is your character's background? Tell us a bit about her.

Donna: Tiny Fists is really powerful, but she doesn't like to show it unless it's absolutely necessary. She likes long walks, bugs called Bob, and exotic holidays.

Reporter: What's her favourite move?

Donna: A fist. In a nostril.

Reporter: That sounds painful.

Donna: Oh, it's not really – look, I'll –

CAN'T WRITE. NOSE TOO SORE. THE REST OF THE INTERVIEW WAS BORING ANYWAY.

The Points Take a Step Back

The mountain rumbled and the mist-covered path groaned as Idabelle came sliding back down it and skidded into the others.

The Scarf Witch materialised in front of them. 'You failed the level two song, so your choices are: go back a level or lose a team member!'

'Team member,' Idabelle said.

The Scarf Witch nodded. 'You must choose one of them – or yourself.'

'Bertha,' Idabelle said, pushing Bertha towards the witch, and with nothing more than a quick zap, Bertha was embroidered on the scarf.

'I can't *believe* you didn't pick Catriona Catcat,'

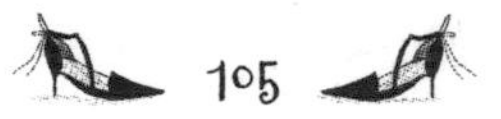

Bertha Bram huffed. Her embroidered mouth rearranged itself into a cross little line.

'We'll get you back at the end,' Idabelle said. 'It just means you won't have to do any work now.'

'Oh yes,' Bertha Bram said, her little embroidered mouth re-stitching itself into a smile. 'That's actually much better. And I have Francesca here to keep me company.'

Idabelle rolled her eyes impatiently. 'Yes, you have Francesca to keep you –' She stopped when she saw the other face. The face had its eyes squeezed shut as if it was trying to hide.

'Peggy Pigwiggle,' Idabelle seethed.

'Our great and powerful Top Witch,' Catriona Catcat said, bowing.

Melodie McDamp kicked her. 'Idabelle will kill you if she sees you respecting the Top Witch!'

Peggy slowly opened her tiny embroidered eyes. 'Oh, um … hello.'

'How did you get here? Why are you here? Is Tiga with you?' Idabelle demanded.

'Talking to contestants from other teams on my scarf is cheating,' the Scarf Witch said. 'You would normally have three tries for this level, but cheats must go back a level.'

The stone game started glowing and Idabelle and her remaining Points were lifted off the ground.

'NO!' Idabelle shouted. 'I wasn't cheating by talking to Peggy! And you've already got Bertha! I WILL NOT GO BACK ANOTHER LEEEEVEEEEEEL.'

She and her fellow Points were thrown back into the lift.

'Back to Under Peak you go,' the Scarf Witch said with a wave.

'Tiga and Fluffanora might have a chance to get ahead now!' Peggy chirped.

'Want a jam star?' Bertha Bram said, as an embroidered tray of treats wove its way along the scarf to Peggy.

☆☆☆

Tiga and Fluffanora stared at the lifts blankly.

'There's no way to know. No clues at all. It's a fifty-fifty chance of getting the right one,' Tiga said, just as there was a *ping* and the doors to the left lift opened.

Catriona Catcat and Melodie McDamp were thrown out, followed by a furious-looking Idabelle Bat.

They stopped and stared at Tiga and Fluffanora.

Tiga and Fluffanora froze.

A witch on a boulder whizzed past. 'Wheeeeeee!' She scooped up Idabelle and the Points and off they trundled back to the start.

'Well, now we know!' Tiga cried, punching the button for the right lift and shoving Fluffanora and the cats inside.

'CURSES!' Idabelle screamed back at them, as the glass lift carried Tiga and Fluffanora off to the next level.

'The right lift was the *right* lift,' Tiga said with a smile. 'It's so simple when you think about it.'

'Tiga,' Fluffanora said, shaking her excitedly. 'Do you know what this means? We're ahead!'

FAIRY FIGHTZ INTERVIEW WITH HYSTERICAL FAN!

Reporter: What do you like most about *Fairy Fightz*, hysterical fan?
Hysterical fan: EEEEESWITS TA BEEEEE YAY! FUN IT GRAWEEEE!
Reporter: I see. And are you going to watch the next episode?
Hysterical fan: SWEEEEEEEEEEEE YA PREEEEEEPTEEE!
Reporter: Of course. And who is your favourite character?
Hysterical fan: GAREEEEEEE YAAAAH. Peanut.

Felicity Bat Reveals All

Back at Linden House, Aggie Hoof watched as Felicity Bat's boot shuffled its way across the floor.

'Are you *sure* it's a boot?' Aggie Hoof asked.

Felicity Bat grunted. She was too busy reading to listen properly.

Aggie Hoof tottered around the boot and unsuccessfully tried to pick it up. 'Fel-Fel, this footwear is strangely heavy.'

'QUIET!' Felicity Bat snapped. 'I'm reading about the ancient jam stores near the top of Pearl Peak! Did you know you can feed ancient jam to *anything* and it will be enjoyed?'

Aggie Hoof stared at her for a second and then slowly stuck her nose in the boot.

She gasped!

'HOW MANY TIMES DO I HAVE TO TELL YOU TO BE QUIET, AG–' Felicity Bat froze and dropped her book. 'The boot … I can … well, I can explain.'

Aggie Hoof slowly backed away from it, her hands raised.

'What *is it*, Fel-Fel?'

'Um,' Felicity Bat said. 'It's a new kind of boot!'

'That's not a boot. Well, the thing in it isn't.'

'No,' Felicity Bat said. 'You're right, it's a –'

'Monster?' Aggie Hoof guessed.

Felicity Bat shook her head.

'Fat ghost?' Aggie Hoof guessed again.

Felicity Bat shook her head.

'A monster?'

'You've guessed that already,' Felicity Bat said, flicking her finger and sending the thing bursting from the boot. It landed with a massive thud on her bed. 'It's a panda.'

'IT'S AS BIG AS A BEAR!' Aggie Hoof screamed. 'What is *pan-da*?'

'It's an animal from the world above the pipes. I saw it on the pile of things the old cart witch had collected last week,' Felicity Bat explained. 'You know, things that have fallen from the pipes. There were nineteen thousand toothbrushes, one squirrel, four hamsters, four hundred hairbands, a shoe, one small briefcase and this panda.'

Aggie Hoof looked sadly at it.

'They're endangered above the pipes, Aggie. I have to return him to the right pipe. I was worried the cart witch might keep him. She only knows how to look after hamsters. And fish.'

Aggie Hoof's eyes welled with tears.

'Don't be sad,' Felicity Bat said. 'We'll return him and everything will be OK.'

'It's not that, Fel-Fel.'

Felicity Bat raised an eyebrow.

'I'm just so sad for panda because he's arrived too late.'

'Pardon?' Felicity Bat said.

'Fel-Fel, he would've matched everything so much better when Sinkville was in black and white. It's so sad. Now he really clashes with the place.'

Felicity Bat flicked her finger and the panda shrank and slipped back into her boot.

'How tragic,' she said faintly.

'When are you going to put him back, Fel-Fel?' Aggie Hoof asked.

'As soon as I find the right pipe,' Felicity Bat said.

Aggie Hoof grinned. 'Can we call him Pandora?'

Felicity Bat pinched the bridge of her nose and exhaled loudly.

'Because is it a panda OR a boot?'

Level Two

The lift opened on to an icy platform that led to an icy path that weaved up and up inside the mountain and disappeared into mist.

Tiga held Fluffanora's hand and the two of them carefully walked forward. The cats were piled on the sled, sleeping. It was the only logical place Tiga could think to put them. Leaving them behind meant they might end up stuck in the mountain, and Peggy seemed quite attached to them.

'This was where we saw Idabelle and the others, when we were right back at the start!' Tiga said, getting down on her knees and smooshing her face against the icy floor. 'Right here!'

Fluffanora yawned. 'Maybe we should stop here for the night. I'm tired and Idabelle is all the way back in the Under Peak. I bet they'll have to do a different challenge this time around, and who knows, they might not even make it here. I'd say we have time for a nap at least.'

Tiga took off her shoe and placed it on the floor.

'Old laces and heels in a heap
Make me a better place to sleep.'

The shoe rose up in the air and –

CRACK!

A giant shoe-shaped house landed with a bang in front of them. Fluffanora stepped inside and began coughing.

'Sorry,' Tiga said as she rearranged the dusty cushions on the sofa. 'I haven't used my boot as a house since Witch Wars, and I haven't cleaned my boots recently either.'

Fluffanora herded the cats upstairs while Tiga peered out of the window.

'Any guesses what's in that mist up ahead?' Tiga called up to Fluffanora.

Fluffanora yawned and flopped on to the dusty bed, flicking her finger and making an eye mask appear on her face. 'I'm not even going to think about that until the morning.'

☆☆☆

Tiga woke up with a cat licking her eyelashes.

Fluffanora was already awake and making them a breakfast of toasted jam, with the remaining jar of Mavis's jam.

Tiga pulled on her one boot and went downstairs. 'Is the mist still there?'

Fluffanora nodded and handed her a splodge of jam.

Tiga gulped it down. 'Well, I suppose we'd better go and see what's waiting for us.'

'Hello?' Tiga whispered as they disappeared into the mist. It was difficult to see the path, so they stuck as close to the wall as they possibly could.

Fluffanora didn't say anything, she just squeezed Tiga's hand tightly.

'It can't just be a treacherous path,' Tiga whispered. 'That would be *too easy*.'

It got darker and the mist grew thicker.

Tiga's stomach flip-flopped with every step she took, and Fluffanora's grip on her hand grew painfully tight.

Then came the buzz.

A ghostly witch appeared in front of them. She floated a little to the left, and made another buzzing sound.

'Did she just buzz?' Tiga whispered. 'Like a bee?'

'I did,' the ghost witch said, sounding bored. 'I went above the pipes and encountered a bee.'

'What's a bee?' Fluffanora said, her eyes wide.

'Nice small things,' Tiga explained quickly. 'They make honey. They sometimes sting if they think you're going to hurt them. Maybe she was allergic to it.'

'So you died because a bee stung you?' Fluffanora asked.

The ghost witch raised a nearly invisible eyebrow. 'No. I tried to run away from it, tripped and fell down a pipe and died that way. The last noise you hear before you die becomes your haunting noise. So I buzz.'

Tiga slyly glanced down at the game in her hand. Their pieces were far up the mountain now, but she could see something new. A musical note.

The ghost buzzed about in front of them, eyeing them suspiciously. 'I can't understand how you two even got past the Mean Lock.'

'Do we have to sing a song?' Tiga asked.

The ghost rolled her almost-invisible eyes. 'Yes, I was just getting to that, if you'd give me a second. I want you to make up a song about bees. And it must end in *buzz*. It's entirely up to me whether the song passes the test.'

'This is silly,' Fluffanora said. 'Plus it's unfair. Of course you're going to say the song isn't good enough, and why does it have to end in *buzz*?'

There was a bang and the Scarf Witch appeared next to them. 'Oh dear,' she said, raising a finger. 'I'm afraid the ghost witch didn't like your song.'

And with a quick flick, Fluffanora was gone. Her face appeared on the scarf, with nice feathers for hair.

'Fluffanora!' Tiga cried.

Her stitched eyes rearranged themselves to look up. 'The feathers are too much! Plus, I didn't even sing a song, I asked a question.'

'You spoke after I had set out the rules, and ended with a buzz,' the ghost witch said. 'I could only assume you were playing the game.'

Tiga stood in silence, trying to process what had just happened. She was on her own. No Peggy, no Fluffanora, just her. And she needed to carry on, she needed to get to the top now more than ever – not only to stop the Ritzy Six, but to save her friends!

'You can do it!' Peggy's sewn little face cheered.

'She can't,' Francesca Fignettle's sequin one sneered.

'If you don't get past this level,' the Scarf Witch said, 'then you all lose.' She tapped an empty patch on the scarf. 'I have a nice little spot for you here.'

Tiga's mind was racing. Why hadn't they asked more witches to come with them? The Points were losing, but there were more of them – they were more likely to reach the top because they had a bigger team.

Tiga began hitting her palm against her forehead.

'You'd better think of a good song,' the ghost witch whispered.

Tiga wanted to tell her she was doing her best, but she was afraid to speak in case she ended up on the scarf.

'You know, this scarf is surprisingly comfy,' Fluffanora said.

'Oh yes,' came the voices from the scarf.

'I HAVE ONE!' Tiga cried. 'It's good.'

They all stared at her. A tiny stitched thumbs up appeared beside Peggy's face.

'If I were a beeeee,
I'd fly straight to Pearl Peak,
And while on my way,
There's one thing I'd saaaaay ...
Buzz.'

Tiga squeezed her eyes shut.

'BRILLIANT!' the ghost witch said with a buzz, and before Tiga knew it she was flying through the air.

'WELL DONE, TIGA!' she heard Fluffanora shout.

'YOU CAN DO IT! YOU'RE ON TO THE NEXT LEVEL!' Peggy cried.

Tiga could feel the cats clinging to her legs.

It was up to her now.

Mavis's Latest Jam Invention

'HAPPY MORNING!' Mavis cried to the gathering crowd. 'And on this fine witchy day, I give you, for the first time ever – PEANUT JAM!' She proudly thrust a jar in their faces.

'Does it taste like peanut? You know, the nuts humans eat?' a witch in the crowd shouted. 'I'm allergic. Because anything touched by a human makes me vomit.'

Mavis chuckled. 'No, no. This jam is filled with strength and sparkle, like Peanut, the star of *Fairy Fightz*.'

A relieved sigh rippled through the crowd.

'I am never inspired by human flavours. I collaborated with the cake team at Cakes, Pies and That's About It

Really to create the flavour, which I'd compare to their pies, but with a dollop of that sweet glittery dust smell.'

The crowd heaved forward, their arms outstretched. Sinkels flew everywhere.

'One at a time, please!' Mavis said. 'One at a time!'

A witch climbed over the stall and grabbed a jar.

Another crowd-surfed to the front and dangled over, grabbing an armful. She was wearing a mask, exactly the same as Peanut's.

'I'M PEANUT'S BIGGEST FAN, I MUST GET AS MANY AS POSSIBLE BEFORE THEY SELL OUT! I DESERVE IT MORE THAN ALL THESE OTHER WITCHES!'

Mavis tried to reason with the crowd.

'Witches, *please*, there is plenty of jam for everyone – and more coming!'

But it was getting out of control. Witches dived behind the stall, pushing Mavis out of the way. By the

JAM

time the crowd had gone, there was nothing left on the stall at all, apart from a few of the aged jams, which no one really liked.

Mavis slumped over her stall and stared at the gigantic pile of sinkels. 'Thank you, the great and glorious Peanut.'

'Wait, why is Peanut great and glorious?' Fran said, buzzing over in her costume.

'Oh, Fran!' Mavis cried. 'Your *Fairy Fightz* character is so popular.'

Fran rolled her eyes. 'Not you as well! Mavis, I'm not Peanut.'

Mavis flashed Fran a knowing smile. 'Oh, don't worry, I know it's just a character you play.'

'But I DON'T play a character called Peanut,' Fran said, but Mavis was already on a roll.

'Fran, I made a jam inspired by Peanut and the whole town has gone crazy! I made more money in the last five minutes than I've made selling jam all year. They completely cleaned out my jam stall.'

She stopped and her eyes grew wide.

'Oh no!' She dived behind the jam stall and emerged seconds later, her face pale.

'They took *a very important jam jar*.'

Fran's beehive flopped.

'Mavis,' she said slowly. 'I've just remembered something. Fluffanora did a temporary spell to make me forget. But it's wearing off!'

'Fran, this isn't the time,' Mavis said, pacing back and forth behind the jam stall, beads of worried sweat dribbling down her forehead.

'I remember everything, Mavis!'

'Very good, Fran, but I'm a little bus –'

'WE DID FILM EPISODE ONE, PART ONE! CRISPY WASN'T LYING!' Fran roared.

Mavis stopped and stared at her. 'That's lovely, Fran. But if you don't mind, I'm closing the jam stall, for the first time ever, as I need to locate a jam jar.'

Fran buzzed in her face and stuck out her legs, lodging a foot in each of Mavis's nostrils.

'Not so fast, Mavis. My newfound memory has just thrown up something interesting that I think you'll want to hear.'

Mavis unplugged the fairy from her nose and set her down on the stall. 'Make it quick.'

'You're worried the crowd have taken your Ritzy Six jam jar. The one with those evil witches inside – the one you've guarded for years.'

Mavis's mouth fell open.

'I know,' Fran said. 'I'm impressive. You see, when I was in the forest, I stumbled upon a Points meeting. I pretended to fly away but I actually hid in the trees, and they had your jam jar. It wasn't the crowd who took it, Mavis. Idabelle Bat did it – days ago.'

Mavis began pacing again. 'She came to see me with her friend Melodie, who is very interested in my cat jam jars.'

'They freed the Ritzy Six, and then they ran off to Pearl Peak.'

Mavis nearly vomited. 'They're going home. I must stop them!'

She froze.

'Peggy,' she said quietly. 'She was headed for Pearl Peak!'

Fran's face fell. 'With my Tiga?'

Mavis nodded gravely.

"Then we will go and get them!' Fran roared. 'YOU, NORMAL MAVIS, AND *ME,* THE ALL-POWERFUL PEANUT!'

Mavis groaned and began walking fast towards Pearl Peak.

'MAVIS, YOU'RE THE SIDEKICK. I MUST LEAD! MAVIS ... ? MAVIS! WAIT FOR ME, MAVIS!'

Mavis stormed on.

'Actually, Mavis,' Fran said quietly, 'I think I might tell Felicity Bat. I'd rather *she* was my sidekick for this one. DID YOU HEAR ME, MAVIS? YOU'RE GETTING VERY CLOSE TO THE MOUNTAIN, MAVIS!'

Gigantico!

Crispy weaved through Brollywood, her nose wobbling as it always did when she was worried.

She flew through the tiny window of Patricia the producer's office and landed on her desk, doing the splits.

Patricia the producer looked up from what she was reading and lowered her glasses. 'Very impressive.'

Crispy turned red in the face and couldn't speak. She gestured at her body and then made a lifting motion.

Patricia the producer lifted her out of the splits.

'Thank you,' Crispy mouthed.

'What did you need to see me about so urgently, Crispy? I prefer witches and fairies to make appointments, rather than buzzing through my window.'

'I can't find her,' Crispy said breathlessly, while trying to click one of her legs back into place. 'Peanut is gone. Again.'

'Well, surely she's somewhere.'

Crispy shook her head. 'Episode two is about to start. The crowds have assembled. She's not in her caravan, the show must go on without her!'

'What do you propose we do?' Patricia the producer asked.

'I have an idea,' Crispy said. 'But I'm not sure you're going to like it.'

☆☆☆

The crowd sat in silent anticipation as Donna, sporting her little hairband with fists on springs, danced around the ring. Julie Jumbo Wings flapped overhead, muttering things about taking over the world and destroying Peanut once and for all.

'BUT!' came Crispy's voice. 'Peanut is an inventive little bean, and she has something big up her sleeve.'

The ground began to rumble. The crowd fell silent.

'SOOOOOMEEEETHIIIIIINNNNGGGGG GIIIIIIIIGGGGAAAAANNNNTTTTTTIIIIC CCCCCOOOOOO!' Crispy yelled, before leaning to the microphone and saying clearly, 'That's Gigantico. A new character called Gigantico.'

Patricia the producer slinked on to set wearing a baggy jumpsuit with tassels along the arms. 'I AM GIGANTICO,' she said awkwardly. 'And Peanut called me in to save the day today.'

The crowd went wild! Someone's sparkly jumpsuit pinged off and hit a fake rainbow hanging overhead. No one seemed to notice.

Julie Jumbo Wings looked like she was going to have a heart attack.

'Crispy,' she hissed. 'The new character is huge.' She narrowed her eyes and gasped when she realised who it was. 'And it's my *BOSS*.'

'Just do the scene as if she was Peanut,' Crispy said.

Julie Jumbo Wings hovered lower. 'Crispy, one of

the moves involves me swinging Peanut around my head.'

'So?' Crispy hissed as Gigantico stepped into the ring and crushed it.

'I can't *swing* her around my head. She's huge, and *my boss*.'

'Improvise,' Crispy said before leaning into the microphone and chanting, 'Gi-gan-ti-co! Gi-gan-ti-co!'

Gigantico picked up Tiny Fists, who muttered something about wanting a raise, and chucked her into the crowd.

The witches roared!

'Gigantico is Peanut's best friend, and together they are unstoppable!' Crispy said. 'Peanut is on holiday in the Cauldron Islands and sent Gigantico in her place – looks like it was a good move!'

'GI-GAN-TI-CO! GI-GAN-TI-CO!' the crowd chanted over and over again.

INTERVIEW WITH GIGANTICO!

Reporter: What do you think your biggest strength is?
Gigantico: The clue is in my name!
Reporter: Ant?
Gigantico: Pardon?
Reporter: The word ant is in your name. Are ants something to do with your strength?
Gigantico: No, it's that I'm gigantic!
Reporter: You're shorter than me.
Gigantico: Yes, but the rest of the cast of *Fairy Fightz* are fairy-sized.
Reporter: That seems a bit unfair. It will be IMPOSSIBLE to defeat you.
Gigantico: Yes ... I'm worried about that. But I'm sure they'll find a way. Hopefully quite soon so I can change out of this jumpsuit.

Reporter: How will they defeat you?
Gigantico: I don't know yet ... you'll have to wait.
Reporter: No, I don't want to wait. Tell me immediately.
Gigantico: No. Even if I did know, I couldn't tell you – that would be a spoiler.
Reporter: You're a spoiler.

Felicity Bat Finds Another Way

Felicity Bat couldn't hear a single word Fran was saying through the frantic wheezing.

'Calm down,' Felicity Bat said, sounding bored. 'I'm sure whatever the problem is, it's not actually a problem.'

Fran stopped and held up a spoon. *Fairy Fightz* was showing.

'I'm missing being the star,' Fran wheezed. '*That* is how important this is.'

'Oh, well, then it must be about Tiga,' Felicity Bat said. 'Go on, indulge me.'

'Ritzy Six,' Fran wheezed. 'They're back. Idabelle. Tiga. The mountain.'

Felicity Bat rose up into the air and levitated over to the window, her heavy boot making her float at an odd angle.

Fran pointed frantically. 'They went inside the mountain, to stop the Ritzy Six.'

'And my big sister brought them back,' Felicity Bat said with a grin.

'PLEASE DON'T TURN EVIL AGAIN!' Fran wailed. 'You're the only one who can help. Mavis is on her way, but she'll never even get past the Mean Lock.'

Felicity Bat rolled her eyes. 'I'm not going to turn evil again. Peggy's well and truly squeezed that out of me with all the hugs and mushy notes she leaves around for me.'

Fran glanced over at the table, where a note with Peggy's bubble writing read *YOU'RE AN AMAZING WITCH, FELICITY! NEVER FORGET IT!*

'Then why were you smiling when I told you about your sister bringing the Ritzy Six back?' Fran asked.

'Because Idabelle is so silly,' Felicity Bat said. 'I bet she thinks she can be friends with the Ritzy Six, or that they'll share their powers. They'll destroy her too.'

'Well then, we should get going,' Fran urged. 'My … sidekick?'

'NO,' Felicity Bat said firmly.

'You'll easily get past the Mean Lock,' Fran said, readjusting her beehive.

'We're not going inside the mountain like everyone else,' Felicity Bat said, crossing her arms. 'We're going to levitate up the side.'

'Can we do that?' Fran asked. 'Isn't it *very* magic, with lots of rules and protection?'

'Have you ever heard of the ancient jam stores near the top of Pearl Peak, Fran?'

Fran nodded. 'They closed them years ago.'

'I've been reading about them recently. And every so often, a witch who could levitate would take the quick route up the side of the mountain to collect the jam.

That was the only witch they let past their defences. Do you know who that witch was?'

'Was she called Sally?' Fran guessed. 'There were a lot of Sallys in the olden days.'

Felicity Bat's face looked strained. 'It was my gran, Fran. Celia Crayfish. I bet the defences would let me past too. We're from the same family, so it's my inheritance. And we can both levitate.'

'It's worth a try!' Fran cheered.

'But you can't come with me,' Felicity Bat said firmly. 'You'd set off alarms. I must do this alone.'

'But the glory,' Fran said. 'Do I still get some of the glory?'

Felicity Bat took off her boot and placed it in front of Fran. 'Better than glory, you get to babysit. I need you to watch my boot until I get back. BUT YOU MUST NOT LOOK INSIDE IT.'

'All right,' Fran said casually as she waved Felicity Bat off. 'I won't look ...'

Tiga Has a Problem

Tiga crash-landed in a small, cave-like room. Little magical lanterns floated about the place and old jam jars littered the floor. There was no door or window. No way in and no way out. Another test. If she failed it, that was it – she and her friends would be trapped in Pearl Peak for ever. As embellishments on a scarf. Probably with Francesca Fignettle and Bertha Bram.

It didn't bear thinking about.

She grabbed a lantern and walked around the room, stopping when she noticed something scratched into the wall:

WELCOME TO LEVEL THREE! THE JAM GOT INTO THE JAM STORE, SO HOW DID IT GET OUT AGAIN?

Tiga slumped in a sad little pile on the floor. 'But how do *I* get out?' she said quietly, just as a cackle came from behind her.

'Looks like you're the only one left,' Idabelle Bat said as she stalked across the room to Tiga. 'And I still have Melodie.'

Melodie blew a bubble.

'What happened to Catriona Catcat?' Tiga asked.

Idabelle shrugged. 'We failed the buzzy witch song the first time around, so on our way back to that level I made Catriona Catcat come up with a brilliant song that would definitely pass the test. Then I stole it and she had no song to sing, so ...'

'She's all made of beads and on a scarf,' Melodie McDamp said.

'And you came up with a good song, too, did you?' Tiga asked Melodie.

Melodie shrugged. 'She seemed to like my rap.'

Tiga edged towards the wall as Idabelle got closer.

'And now it's just us,' she said with a sinister grin. 'Did you really think you'd reach the top before us? And even if you did, what were you going to do – take on the Ritzy Six all by yourself?'

Tiga blinked. She hadn't really thought that far ahead.

Idabelle cackled. 'No! I thought not.'

'Well, it doesn't matter,' Tiga said. 'We're all stuck in this room – and if one of us figures out how to get out, then the others will see it and we'll all get out. We'll reach the top at exactly the same time!'

Idabelle wandered over to the wall and began flicking jam jars out of the way.

'What are you doing?' Tiga asked, edging closer.

Melodie blew a bubble, but this time it flew from her mouth and began floating over the jars. It stopped and popped above a particularly dusty one.

Idabelle grabbed it and threw off the lid. 'Of course,' she said, holding up a key. Before Tiga knew what was happening, the key connected to the wall with a *clang* and Idabelle pulled at it. The wall opened like a zip! She kept going in a loop until one side of the room unzipped completely and fell away.

They stood back and stared at the hole she had uncovered. The freezing wind whipped Tiga's hat off. She leaned down to pick it up, feeling slightly relieved that even if she couldn't beat the Ritzy Six, she could at the very least save her friends.

Idabelle stared at the hole.

'You know what, Tiga, you were right. We'll *all* make it to the top now, at almost the exact same time. And you've played really well for such a young and inexperienced witch. Obviously you'll never beat us or the Ritzy Six, but at the very least you deserve to have your friends back.'

Idabelle gave Melodie McDamp a leg up and she climbed out of the hole. 'It'll just be a quick climb. Come on, Tiga, let me help you.'

Tiga smiled and placed her foot in Idabelle's hands.

'Stick your head out of the hole,' Idabelle said.

Tiga did, as sprinkles of Pearl Peak snow tickled her face. She closed her eyes and sighed. Her friends would be saved!

'Thank you, Ida–'

She felt Idabelle's hand shove her and before she could grab on to anything, her whole body lurched forward. She spun, free-falling fast through the air.

'Don't worry!' Idabelle called down to her. 'The Scarf Witch won't let you hit the bottom – she'll magic your little face on to her scarf before you do!'

She cackled.

'Enjoy living in Pearl Peak for ever!'

Tiga let out a scream, but she was falling so fast the wind gobbled it up. She could feel her cheeks sticky with tears. She squeezed her eyes shut, wishing for it to be over. She'd failed everyone!

She stopped.

She could feel hands on her ankles, holding her

tightly, and slowly she opened her eyes. The Scarf Witch had claimed her prize.

But it wasn't the Scarf Witch.

'I told you not to go to the Points gathering,' Felicity Bat whispered.

Mavis and the Mean Lock

Mavis stood before the black iron gates at the base of Pearl Peak Mountain, begging.

'Oh, please let me in. I have heard you're a Mean Lock, so I'd just like to say, I am *very* mean.'

The gates groaned, but they didn't open.

Mavis leaned in closer and whispered. 'Do you like … jam? I could provide you with some special *free* jam. Oh no, of course you don't care about that! You're a *gate*!'

FAIRY FIGHTZ INTERVIEW WITH CRISPY!

Reporter: Crispy, you are the behind-the-scenes fairy, the one who makes it all happen. How are you enjoying *Fairy Fightz* so far?

Crispy: Aside from constantly losing Peanut, I quite enjoy it. It's nice to see fairies in fun and different roles, rather than being all sweet and glittery. I've always been a big champion of letting fairies be fairies, and wear and do what they want. Sometimes witches look at me funnily because I'm not shooting glittery dust or smiling.

Reporter: You've got quite an angry face, too. More troll-like.

Crispy: I take that as a compliment. I really like my face.
Reporter: And I really like YOU, Crispy.
Crispy: Great.

Peanut Returns

Patricia the producer strutted around the ring dressed as Gigantico, baring her teeth at the crowds.

'She's got way too into this,' Julie Jumbo Wings said. 'I'm never going to be able to take her seriously again.'

'Are we doing *another* episode without Peanut?' Donna asked. 'It was more fun with Peanut. Gigantico could actually kill me.'

Crispy clapped her hands. 'Less talking about Peanut, more whipping up the crowds, please! We go live in one minute – take your places!'

Donna lay down and fell asleep, while Julie Jumbo Wings hid behind one of the fake rainbows.

'Three! Two! One! And action!' Crispy shouted before putting on her deep announcer voice. 'IN THE FAIRY REALMS, THE GREAT AND POWERFUL GIGANTICO HAS PROVED UNSTOPPABLE! THE FAIRIES COWER, THEY HIDE, THEY –'

Julie Jumbo Wings burst from behind a rainbow.

'IT'S FLAPPY!' Crispy cried, just as Gigantico waved a hand and sent Flappy somersaulting off into the distance, hitting a couple of witches in the crowd as she went.

Everyone fell silent.

Donna opened one eye. 'Gigantico wasn't meant to do that.'

'I thought she was approaching from my left, my *left*,' Gigantico whispered to Crispy.

'Just carry on,' Crispy hissed. 'I'll improvise.'

She cleared her throat.

'GIGANTICO HAS WON! THERE IS NO FAIRY THAT CAN DEFEAT HER! *FAIRY FIGHTZ* IS HER DOMAIN! HER WORLD! HER –'

'IS THAT A *PANDA*?!' someone from the crowd screamed, as Fran came cantering into the ring.

The panda reared, with Fran strapped to its back.

'PEANUT RETURNS!' Fran cried, as the panda lunged at Gigantico and flattened her.

Crispy winced. Peanut bowed. Gigantico muttered something angry from underneath the panda.

THE CROWD WENT WILD!

'PEA-NUT! PEA-NUT! PEA-NUT!'

Peanut lifted up one of the Panda's paws to reveal Gigantico looking furious.

'Patricia the producer, can I just say, you have done a wonderful job filling in for me. I'm sorry about the panda. But it was entirely necessary.'

'Where did you get a panda?' Patricia the producer hissed. 'It looks expensive.'

'Oh, don't worry! It was free!' Fran said, stroking Patricia the producer's face and making her turn a furious shade of purple. 'I found it in a boot.'

The Top of Pearl Peak

The house that balanced on the very tip of Pearl Peak was small and solid and had seven crooked windows – one on the ground floor and six on the second floor. In the six windows Tiga could just make out the faces of the Ritzy Six.

Felicity Bat set Tiga down on the mountain and the pair of them crouched beneath the ledge of the peak.

'They each have a special power. More powerful than any witch before them. Idabelle has wanted one for years.'

'Air, fire, water, earth, jam and hair,' Tiga listed efficiently.

She could see Idabelle dancing at the door of the house.

'Can you let us in?' Idabelle oozed. 'Have you collected everything you need to wreak havoc? Can you teach me your tricks now?'

Felicity Bat groaned. 'She's gone off the rails.'

Francesca Fignettle, Bertha Bram and Catriona Catcat were back, which gave Tiga a smidgen of relief – at least the Scarf Witch was honest. Now she just had to make sure she got to the Peak.

The door to the house burst open and One, Two and Three emerged, followed by Four, Five and Six.

'They've had a costume change,' Tiga whispered.

'What?' Felicity Bat hissed.

'Costume change,' Tiga said again. 'When your sister brought them back they were wearing twig and leaf dresses. Now, well –'

'Sparkly jumpsuits,' Felicity Bat said. 'What's your point? That's what they always wore in the olden days. They must've had spares locked in their house.'

They watched as the Ritzy Six began talking in whispers to Idabelle.

'What are they saying?' Felicity Bat said. 'Can you hear them?'

'I need to climb up just a smidge further,' Tiga said, gripping the snow. 'I need to save Fluffanora and Peggy from the scarf before we do anything else.'

'Wait,' Felicity Bat said.

But Tiga had already launched herself on to the peak.

'Why wait?' she whispered back down to Felicity Bat, just as the heel of her left boot hit the snow.

BANG!

'That's why,' Felicity Bat groaned, as the Points and the Ritzy Six snapped around to see where the bang had come from.

The smoke cleared and the Scarf Witch coughed loudly. 'Well done,' she said flatly, taking the stone game from Tiga's pocket and handing her the scarf.

There was another *BANG* and a slight *TWANG* and Fluffanora and Peggy were back.

'YOU DID IT!' Fluffanora cried. 'Oh, when

Francesca Fignettle, Bertha Bram and Catriona Catcat were freed, we thought something terrible had happened to you.'

'Now what?' Peggy said as someone coughed loudly behind them.

They turned slowly to see the Ritzy Six and the Points lined up and looking angry.

Six cackled and blinked. Peggy's hair pinged into a spiky Mohawk.

'Wow,' Felicity Bat said sarcastically.

Six cackled and blinked again.

Felicity Bat's hat went flying off, along with her hair. A single curl pinged about at the front of her head, poking her in the eye.

'Better,' Felicity Bat said, flicking her finger. Her hat landed back on her head. 'Is that the best you can do? We witches are a lot more advanced these days.'

'Stop taunting them,' Tiga pleaded.

One raised her hands in the air and the winds picked up, sending the three of them stumbling backwards.

'She controls the wind, and she's too powerful!' Peggy cried.

Felicity Bat leapt up and waved her hand. The wind slowed, but not enough.

Idabelle cackled. 'Oh, look, my little sister. Felicity, when will you realise, I don't want to hang out with you.'

'Oh, go away, Idabelle,' Felicity Bat snapped back.

'Gladly,' Idabelle said as Four stomped hard on the ground. The mountain began to rumble. The Ritzy Six and the Points disappeared in a puff of smoke.

'WHERE HAVE THEY GONE?!' Tiga cried.

She watched as Felicity Bat levitated higher.

The spindly tip of Pearl Peak was wobbling in the wind.

'WHAT ARE YOU DOING?' she called up to her.

Felicity Bat levitated back down to them and landed with a thud. 'The tip of the mountain is going to break off. Hold on to my legs.'

'You can't carry all three of us on your legs,' Fluffanora scoffed.

Felicity Bat fixed her with a determined stare.

'Fluffanora, I have been carrying a panda around in my boot all week. Trust me, I can HANDLE IT.'

Tiga grabbed Felicity Bat's leg and was hoisted in the air. Fluffanora jumped and grabbed on to Tiga and with a wobbly leap, Peggy jumped as high as she could.

Then, from out of nowhere, jam exploded everywhere, splatting Peggy back on to the mountain and covering her from head to toe.

Tiga could just make out two eyes blinking in the huge pile of old jam.

'The ancient jam stores are exploding!' Felicity Bat shouted. 'COME ON, PEGGY!'

Peggy ripped her way out of the jam pile like a hero and took a deep breath.

'JUMP!' Felicity Bat roared, as Tiga squeezed her eyes shut. 'QUICKLY!'

The tip of the mountain broke away!

Peggy tumbled out of sight!

Felicity Bat closed her eyes and let out an impatient sigh. 'If everyone just did what I *said*.'

'Well, catch her then!' Fluffanora demanded.

Peggy was still somersaulting through the air as Felicity Bat levitated down to reach her.

'Sorry!' Peggy said, her nose stuffed with jam. She sneezed, sending a splatter of it over Felicity Bat.

Fluffanora held her leg out and Peggy grabbed on.

'You're covered in jam!' Tiga laughed.

'I'll eat it off and I bet I can finish before we reach the bottom!' Peggy joked.

'You're such a glass-half-full witch, aren't you?' Felicity Bat said, just as the bunch of cats leapt on to Peggy and began madly licking the jam.

'Now, let's go back to Ritzy City and catch some witches!' Peggy cheered.

'But how? There are so many of them compared to us,' Tiga said, sounding worried. 'And they have special powers!'

Felicity Bat cackled. 'Did you see the sparkly jump-suits they were wearing? They'll stick out like jam thumbs and every witch in town will help us stop them.'

More Giganticos!

When they arrived back in Ritzy City, hundreds of witches were wearing sparkly jumpsuits.

'I'M GIGANTICO!' a witch said proudly.

Six ran past her.

'OH, I LIKE YOUR OUTFIT, WHICH ONE OF THE *FAIRY FIGHTZ* CAST ARE YOU?' a witch called over.

'Six,' Six grunted before disappearing into the crowds again.

'I haven't heard of Six ... I MUST'VE MISSED AN EPISODE!' the witch wailed. She charged off, sending *Fairy Fightz* fans flying as she went.

'Who is Gigantico?' Tiga asked as Crispy came buzzing over.

'Patricia the producer is Gigantico,' Crispy said.

'Patricia the producer plays a character in *Fairy Fightz*?' Tiga said, looking down the street.

Crispy nodded. 'She's broken the set four times with her witch-sized feet.'

'And the witches are dressed as her because …'

'She's a HUGE hit!' Crispy said. 'But not as huge as –'

'PAAAAANDAAAAAAA!' a witch cried as she cantered past dressed as one.

Felicity Bat's eyes widened. 'FRAAAAAAAN!' she roared, making the lamp posts shake.

'So witches all over Sinkville are dressed in sparkly jumpsuits,' Tiga said in disbelief.

'Almost everyone,' Crispy said proudly.

Felicity Bat put her head in her hands and let out a muffled scream.

Crispy flew off.

'I *knew* she'd look in the boot,' Felicity Bat seethed.

Fran trotted past slowly on the panda.

When she spotted Felicity Bat she stood up tall on its back. 'I was just –' she began, but Felicity Bat flicked her finger before she could finish and off the panda soared, back towards Linden House and the boot.

Tiga's mouth fell open.

Fran hit the ground with a bang.

'YES, FINE, ALL RIGHT, I ADMIT IT!' Felicity Bat roared. 'I HAD A PANDA IN MY BOOOOOOOOT!'

'Ah,' Peggy said. 'That's why it was heavy.' She leaned over and closed Tiga's mouth.

'Pandora!' they heard Aggie Hoof cry from the crowds. 'You're FLYING!'

Fran shot off in a huff.

'What now?' Felicity Bat snapped. 'The Ritzy Six don't stand out in their weird outfits, they blend right in. We'll never stop them. And Fran showed people my PANDA!'

Mavis came racing up, her eyes growing wide when

she saw what all the witches were wearing. 'YOU HAVE *GOT* TO BE JOKING!'

Down the street, Two used her special fire power to set light to Brew's, while Three flicked her finger and burst some of the pipes above Linden House.

'Wow!'

'Whoa!'

'Toads!' witches cried with delight.

'It must be new characters from *Fairy Fightz*!'

'This is giving me flashbacks of the time One lifted me on to the top of the Ritzytwig Theatre and everyone thought it was a show,' Mavis said. 'I won four awards.'

A huge ball of jam flew through the air and splatted on Tiga. Five waved at her from the crowd and then skipped off.

Tiga clenched her fists. 'Let's get those witches back in the jam jar, Mavis.'

'Who has the jam jar?' Mavis whispered. 'Or should I get a new one? I suppose it doesn't need to be the same jam jar.'

Tiga closed her eyes and said faintly, 'Any jam jar is *fine*, Mavis. Thank you.'

☆☆☆

It turned out it was really difficult to round up six witches with special powers.

Tiga and the others grouped together in the middle of Ritzy Avenue. Peggy was snuffing out the fire on her skirt. Fluffanora was covered in mud and Felicity Bat and Mavis were wearing head-to-toe jam.

Tiga stood in the middle of them, completely soaked. Idabelle raced past cackling, 'The Points win!'

Six tapped Tiga on the shoulder and grinned. 'There you are!' she cried, but Six flicked her finger and sent Tiga flying backwards.

'Oh dear,' Mavis said, pointing at Tiga's hair.

Tiga felt the top of her head.

'Ah,' she said. 'I seem to have hair horns.'

Then she saw that Fluffanora's hair was entirely made of feathers, Peggy's was so long that she tripped and

rolled over it, Mavis was a classic bald and Felicity Bat had little baby pigtails with huge bows.

Another huge splodge of jam fell from the air and covered them.

Idabelle danced past again. 'Had enough yet? You've lost, Felicity! You've lost, Tiga!' She ran for Linden House and dived through one of the windows. 'And now we take control!'

The Ritzy Six and the remaining Points followed her, apart from Bertha Bram, who was lying in a puddle of jam, lapping it up with her tongue like a cat.

Felicity Bat stepped over her and stared at Linden House, her tiny pigtails wafting in the wind.

'This is where it ends,' she said firmly.

'HELP!' came Fran's voice from one of the windows in Linden House. Six pasted the tiny fairy up against the window and wiped her across it, like a really ineffective window cleaner.

'IT'S PEANUT!' the crowd cried. 'THIS MUST

BE A SPECIAL SHOW! THE NEW CHARACTERS HAVE PEANUT!'

'IT'S REAL!' Tiga cried, but no one was listening. She turned to Felicity Bat. 'Why would they capture Fran?'

Felicity Bat bit her lip. 'The thing is,' she said, talking fast. 'Back in the day, the Ritzy Six were convinced that all they had to do to be immortal was to eat a fairy. But then they got stuffed in a jam jar, so ...'

'WHAT?' Tiga cried, racing towards her fairy. 'We've got to save her!'

The crowd mushroomed around Linden House, standing on each other's shoulders and doing quick spells to make themselves taller to get the best view. There were pops and bangs and flashes of magic.

'We'll go in the back,' Felicity Bat said as they sidestepped around the crowds.

The Ultimate Fairy Snack

Tiga could see Six standing with Fran in the middle of the Linden House sitting room. The others were lazing on the sofas, along with Idabelle and the Points. Catriona Catcat was skipping on the spot, chanting, 'PO-WER! PO-WER!'

The crowd outside started chanting the same.

Tiga rolled her eyes. 'I can't believe they think it's a show!'

'I'M NOT ACTING!' Fran cried. 'CAN'T YOU TELL? NO, OF COURSE YOU CAN'T, BECAUSE I AM THAT GOOD AN ACTOR! BUT I'M NOT ACTING THIS TIME – I NEED HELP!'

'YOU CAN DO IT, PEANUT!' a witch from the crowd shouted.

'I CAN'T!' Fran called back. 'I AM IN A VICE-LIKE GRIP.'

'PEA-NUT! PEA-NUT! PEA-NUT!' the crowd roared.

Tiga and the others took their chance and scuttled across the room, ducking behind one of the sofas.

Melodie McDamp sniffed the air and blew a large bubble.

'She can smell us,' Tiga whispered as the bubble popped, making Mavis scream.

Idabelle whipped around. 'Well, come on out, don't hide.'

Mavis popped up from behind the sofa, pushing the others down. 'Oh hello, I am obviously in the wrong place … I was just delivering the latest jam to the Top Witch, but I … can't find her, so …'

'Terrible liar,' Felicity Bat whispered. 'Idabelle won't be fooled.'

'A jam delivery?' Idabelle said with a smirk. 'Well, Peggy doesn't need any jam, because Five here can make as much jam as Ritzy City needs with a magic flick of the finger. Your stall will be useless. No one will visit it.'

Two flicked her finger and just outside the window, behind the roaring crowds, Mavis's jam stall burst into flames.

Mavis put her head in her hands. 'You know, I'd like there to be just one Tiga adventure when my jam stall did not *break*.'

'Oops,' Idabelle said.

Felicity Bat flicked her finger and a stream of water fell from a pipe above, putting out the flames.

'Hey!' Idabelle cried. 'Who did that?'

She stopped and growled.

'*I know*.'

'Why did you do that?' Tiga whispered.

'It's Mavis's *dream*, Tiga. Have a heart,' Felicity Bat hissed, just as her sister jumped up on the sofa and leaned over.

'AHA! I KNEW IT!'

Tiga, Felicity Bat, Fluffanora and Peggy rose to their feet.

'Nice hair,' Francesca Fignettle said genuinely. 'My spirit fly is jealous of you all.'

'HELP!' Fran squealed.

'We're trying,' Tiga said, as One, Two, Three, Four and Six circled them.

'What are they going to do?' Fluffanora said, hiding behind Peggy's extra-long curtains of hair.

'We're going to eat her,' Six said with a smirk.

Fran gulped. 'Her as in … me?'

Six nodded.

'Wait a second,' Two said. 'If you eat that fairy, then *you* become immortal. What about us?'

'You should share her!' Three shouted. 'We each get a bit!'

Fran grabbed hold of her beehive.

'You need to eat the *whole* fairy,' Six snapped.

Four threw her hands in the air. 'Who says *you* get to eat it?'

'Me!' Six screamed. 'Because I'm in charge!'

'YEAH!' Idabelle shouted. 'GO, SIX!'

'I'm so sick of you,' Six grumbled, sending Idabelle crashing through the window and into the crowds outside.

Tiga saw Felicity Bat quickly flick her finger, breaking Idabelle's fall.

'Who did that?' Idabelle shouted. 'Who made me float like that?' But the crowd swallowed her up with hugs and shouts of 'BRAVO!'

'EXCELLENT SPECIAL EFFECTS!' a witch outside shouted, staring in awe at the broken window.

'NOW STAND BACK!' Six said, holding up Fran. 'I have waited a long time for this moment.'

'YAY!' someone from the crowd shouted.

She opened her mouth wide.

'WAIT!' Fran cried. 'I HAVE FRIENDS!'

Everyone in the room stopped.

They turned to look at Fran.

And so did everyone outside.

'Oh, *now* we're her friends,' Julie Jumbo Wings said. 'Did she write this into the script?'

'I don't think this is a show,' Crispy whispered.

'LOOK!' Fran shouted. 'THERE THEY ARE! Now if you find Donna as well – she's always walking so is less easy to spot – then *four* of you could become immortal. Or three of you, if you chose to save me because I've been so kind in telling you about some of my friends that you could eat.'

'Fran!' Tiga cried in outrage.

Fran rolled her eyes. 'OK, you can perhaps eat a *little* corner of my beehive. As long as you promise to pay for my hairdressing bill.'

Felicity Bat's eyes darted from the crowds to the Ritzy Six to Fran and back again.

'She's trying to get us eaten,' Julie Jumbo Wings said to Crispy.

Six nodded at the crowd. 'Well, if you others want a fairy, then go get them. I've got mine.'

She opened her mouth wide again.

'NOT PEANUUUUUT!' the crowd cried. '*NOT* PEANUT!'

She stopped and stared at them '*Who* is *Peanut*?'

'The shoe,' Fran mouthed at Tiga. 'Get the boot.'

'I think she wants new boots,' Peggy whispered.

Tiga dived to the floor. She knew what Fran wanted her to do! She grabbed Felicity Bat's heavy boot.

'Six!' she shouted. 'Catch!'

Everything seemed to go in slow motion – Six looked up as the boot tumbled towards her. Felicity Bat turned slowly, watching the boot go. Six reached out a hand, closer and closer, and then –

THWUNK!

'YES!' Tiga roared.

With the panda inside, the boot was so heavy that Six tipped straight over, just like a bug on an aggressive seesaw. Fran sprang from her other hand, went flying across the room and hit the wall with a *splat*.

The crowd went wild!

'NOOOOOOW!' Fluffanora roared, grabbing Peggy's long hair and lassoing the Ritzy Six in a nice tight knot.

Mavis pulled a jam jar from her pocket and threw it through the broken window. Only it missed the broken one and shattered the one beside it.

'EXCELLENT SPECIAL EFFECTS!' the witch in the crowd shouted again.

Felicity Bat grabbed the jam jar and began to mutter a spell.

'Wait,' Idabelle said. 'How do you know the spell to put them back in the jam jar?'

'Because she's now read every book in the Linden House library,' Peggy said. 'Apart from the Batty Boo series, because she's not interested in a bat-loving witch. She's definitely seen that jam jar spell somewhere.'

'NOOOOOOOO!' the Ritzy Six wailed as they were sucked towards the jam jar – apart from Two, who chirped, 'BYE AGAIN!'

A second later, they were gone.

Mavis dived through the window and screwed on the lid as Felicity Bat landed in an exhausted heap on the floor.

Tiga knelt down and put Felicity Bat's heavy boot back on her foot.

'Thanks,' Felicity Bat said, getting to her feet. 'Now I've got something important to take care of. I have a panda to return to the world above the sink pipes. And please can someone arrange to pay him for his work on *Fairy Fightz* before we leave?'

'What does she mean?' Mavis whispered.

'And I do not expect to have to save the day *ever* again,' Felicity Bat snapped, before levitating out of the window.

A dishevelled-looking Idabelle leapt from the crowd and tried to grab Felicity by the boot, but even when she was lopsided, she still levitated too high. 'You meddling little witch!' she shouted after her before turning her attention to Tiga.

'You, Tiga,' Idabelle shouted through the window, 'ARE DEFINITELY *NOT* IN THE POINTS!'

Tiga smiled and linked arms with Peggy and Fluffanora. 'Why would I want to be?'

'Come *on*, Points!' came Idabelle's furious shout from outside the window.

Catriona Catcat, Francesca Fignettle and Bertha Bram looked at her and then scuttled over to Melodie McDamp.

Melodie blew another bubble. 'What?'

'Looks like you're in charge of the Points now,' Tiga said with a smile.

Meanwhile, outside, the crowd was going wild, high-fiving Peanut as she soared above them.

'I WON!' Fran cried, smooshing herself against the window. 'I DEFEATED THE MOST EVIL WITCHES FROM SINKVILLE'S HISTORY – THE RITZY SIX ARE NO MATCH FOR PEEEEEANUUUUT!'

'PEA-NUT! PEA-NUT! PEA-NUT!' the crowd cheered.

'I wonder what Fran would taste like,' Peggy said.

'Chewy,' Fluffanora said. 'And arrogant.'

'I bet she goes well with jam,' Peggy joked. And they burst into a fit of giggles.

Witches Together

'It's time for a new episode of *FAIRY FIGHTZ*!' Crispy's voice boomed from the spoon. 'Just to confirm, the *incident* at Linden House yesterday was *not* an episode, it really was Fran almost being eaten by the Ritzy Six. BUT BACK TO THE SHOW!'

'I can see why witches are going crazy for this!' Tiga said to Mavis, as Peanut flew into the ring and kissed the camera lens.

'Don't kiss the lens,' they heard Crispy hiss. 'It smudges it.'

A tiny finger wiped the screen and the ring came back into view.

'Peanut avoided being eaten by some new and

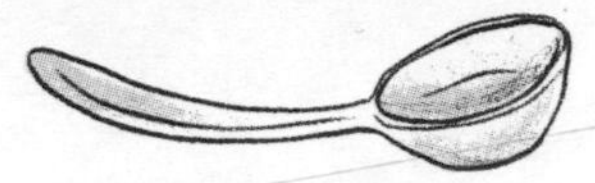

mysterious characters who probably won't be in the show again for quite complicated reasons, but now she has been reunited with her sidekick, GIGANTICO!'

Patricia the producer marched on to the set with her fringed jumpsuit, squashing the ring completely.

'Will Tiny Fists and Flappy ever be able to stop them?'

Tiga put the spoon away and said goodbye to Mavis. She grabbed a pot of jam, then ran up the steps to Linden House and rang the bell.

'Sleepover time!' Peggy said as she threw the door open. Fluffanora was already there with a tray of Clutterbucks cocktails.

They sneaked upstairs and along the corridor to Felicity Bat's room.

'SURPRISE SLEEPOVER!' Tiga cried as they burst in.

Felicity Bat put down the Batty Boo book she was reading and glared up at them. 'I don't do sleepovers.'

'Yes you do!' Peggy said, jumping into the bed next to her.

Felicity Bat tried not to smile.

Tiga pulled a tiny toy panda from her jacket. 'Fluffanora made it for you.'

'I knew you wouldn't want one of my outfit designs,' Fluffanora said with a smile.

'I'M HERE, FEL-FEL!' came a cry, and Aggie Hoof cantered into the room. She dumped a pile of old *Toad* magazines on the floor.

Fluffanora picked one up and began flicking through it.

Felicity Bat grabbed two Clutterbucks cocktails and handed one to Tiga.

'We've come a long way since the Witch Wars days,' Peggy said. 'Remember when we all fought against each other?'

'It was the competition,' Felicity Bat said. 'It wasn't nice to pit us against each other.'

'But we knew better,' Tiga said. 'And look at us now – looking out for each other.'

Felicity Bat gulped down a spoonful of jam. 'It's like that old Witchoween chant: WITCHES TOGETHER ARE STRONGER THAN SPELLS.'

Fran shot through the door and dunked herself in Tiga's Clutterbucks cocktail. 'Witches together are *not* stronger than Peanut. My character in *Fairy Fightz* will go down as the strongest character of all time.'

They laughed.

Tiga smiled and raised her Clutterbucks. 'Very well. WITCHES TOGETHER ARE STRONGER THAN SPELLS, BUT NOT STRONGER THAN PEANUT FROM *FAIRY FIGHTZ*.'

'*See*,' Fran said. 'Now *that's* catchy.'

Read on for a peek at
the first fabulously fishy book in the
BAD MERMAIDS series

AVAILABLE NOW!

Prologue

Mermaids have been flopping all over this planet for a really long time. And yet no submarine, ship or sinking scientist has ever discovered their whopping world.

Only mermaids know how to get to the Hidden Lagoon. Deep down beneath the waves, just past the NO LEGS BEYOND THIS POINT sign, is a small shell, and inside that shell is a keypad made of old pearly buttons. To open the gates to the Lagoon and all the cities within it, all you have to do is type in the secret code. The code that for thousands of years has kept mermaids hidden from human sight –

The unbreakable!

The UNFAKEABLE!

Ihavenolegs.

1

In a Fish Tank on Land

'May I borrow a pen please?'

'A pen?' an excitable lady squawked, waving her arms elaborately like someone swatting at least forty flies. She tottered over to the fish tank, her large feet clad in spotted socks and squeezed into a pair of stilettos.

'Yes please, a pen,' came the tired voice from somewhere in the tank's murky water. An elegant hand, fingers adorned with pearl and crystal rings and a wrist stacked with swirly shell bracelets, flopped out of the tank.

'WE'RE COMMUNICATING!' the excitable lady wheezed with joy. She tossed a pen into the tank. 'Me and you. You and me. You and your fin. Me and my socks.'

There was a sigh from inside the tank.

'I heard that!' the excitable lady snapped. 'I've

installed very
sensitive microphones
in that tank.'

There was a deliberately loud burp.

'*And that*,' the excitable lady groaned. 'Oh, I can't wait to show you to the world! I'll be famous. They won't believe how I got you! NOW GIVE THE PEN BACK.' She banged on the glass before reaching a hand in and wrenching the pen from the mermaid's grasp. 'You're *mine* now, Arabella Cod.'

'No!' Arabella Cod gasped. 'I hadn't finished!'

The excitable lady squealed as she caught a flash of pearly fin. 'What did you write?!'

'Nothing,' Arabella Cod said quickly. 'I ... just wanted to hold it.'

The excitable lady twirled around the room, laughing uncontrollably. 'WHAT A DAY!' she roared, punching the air. 'ARABELLA COD, THE MERMAID QUEEN, MY PRISONER FOREVER!' A tiny crab hastily heaved itself out of the tank and scuttled quickly along behind her, carrying a sloppy lump of seaweed.

The excitable lady twirled in its direction.

It froze.

She twirled on her heel once more to face the tank, peering eagerly inside and stroking the glass affectionately. The crab took its chance and scuttled out of the door.

'Don't stop until you get there!' Arabella Cod shouted after it. 'I'm sure they'll figure it out! They have to ...'

The excitable lady turned to the door. But the crab was gone.

'Who on *earth* are you shouting at, you strange lump of fish?' she spat.

But Arabella Cod said nothing.

Failing to see that crab would be the biggest mistake the excitable lady ever made.

2

Crabagram!

'CRABAGRAM!' Beattie roared as she slipped her feet into a pair of purple wedges and clattered out of the door, letting it bang loudly behind her. Her friends Zelda and Mimi were sprawled on the sofa, napping. On a night like this! It was just like them to be dribbling and snoring away on *crabagram* night.

She raced along the promenade, the warm Californian breeze whipping about her plaited hair. She took it all in. The jingle of shop doors closing, the smell of hot pavements and plastic pool toys.

'Nice night for a run!' a girl called out from the little lopsided ice-cream stall that sat in front of an old, sprawling factory. Her creamy complexion was decorated with swirls of sunburn. She waved a

clawlike hand, bent from constantly holding ice-cream cones.

Beattie smiled and waved back as she tore along the wooden pier, each faded plank decorated with carvings and doodles – names, insults, a little crab drawing Beattie had carved on her first day there. She leapt and landed in the soft sand, plonked herself down and pulled her skirt over her temporary knees.

It wasn't there. Not yet.

'Well, I tell you, I can't wait to get rid of these cumbersome bananas!' Zelda said, slapping her legs and making Mimi snort. Zelda had got into the habit of using human words like banana to incorrectly describe stuff like legs. 'And I've only had the bananas for two weeks.'

The two of them joined Beattie on the beach, sloppy hotdogs in hand. Although they were twins, they looked nothing alike. Mimi was the shorter of the two, clad in gold sandals and topped with messy hair pulled into two loose plaits.

'Well, hello there, good sir,' she said, nodding at a folded sun lounger.

Beattie and Zelda both stared blankly at her.

'What?' Mimi whispered. 'You don't know what can hear you on land.'

'Usually just the stuff with ears,' Zelda whispered back, taking a big bite of her hotdog and sending a spray of mustard on to her ripped jeans.

Zelda was taller, with short, perfectly groomed hair, flicked for effect, and eyes so packed with mischief her eyelids looked like they were straining to contain it all. Her nails were short, bitten obsessively. Beattie had known them both forever and the three of them did everything together, which was why Beattie had managed to convince them to do a summer on land, with legs.

'Where's the crabagram?' Beattie said, pacing back and forth by the water's edge.

Zelda looked at Mimi, who poured some sand on her hotdog and took a bite.

'That's not what humans put on hotdogs,' said Zelda.

Mimi eagerly dipped her hotdog in the sand and took another bite. 'If I could, I'd tell the humans that sand is the ketchup of the sea! But then they'd know I was a mermaid, so I can't.'

'Wait,' Beattie said, squinting in the darkness. 'There it is!'

Zelda rolled her eyes. 'I've never seen someone so excited to read *Clamzine*.'

Beattie waved a hand dismissively. 'It's our only link to home right now, *Zelda*. And my mum's latest adventure article will be in it!'

A crab scuttled up the beach, wonkily and with urgency, holding a chunk of seaweed carefully like it was cradling a sloppy baby. It placed it gently on Beattie's big toe.

'Thank you, madam,' she said, yanking the loose sheets of seaweed out of the slippery envelope.

'Dive into a fin-tastic, madcap adventure that's funnier than being tickled by a giant octopus!'
Award-winning author David Solomons on Bad Mermaids
BLOOMSBURY
SIBÉAL POUNDER
BAD Mermaids
Illustrated by Jason Cockcroft
SIBÉAL POUNDER
BAD Mermaids
On the Rocks
Illustrated by Jason Cockcroft
BLOOMSBURY
AVAILABLE NOW!

WITCH WARS
Read the whole ritzy, glitzy, witchy series!
SIBÉAL POUNDER
WITCH WARS
A WITCH WARS ADVENTURE
SIBÉAL POUNDER
WITCH SWITCH
A WITCH WARS ADVENTURE